MURDER STALKS CHRISTMAS

Rooftop Garden Cozy Mysteries, Book 15

THEA CAMBERT

Summer Prescott Books Publishing

Copyright 2022 Summer Prescott Books

All Rights Reserved. No part of this publication nor any of the information herein may be quoted from, nor reproduced, in any form, including but not limited to: printing, scanning, photocopying, or any other printed, digital, or audio formats, without prior express written consent of the copyright holder.

**This book is a work of fiction. Any similarities to persons, living or dead, places of business, or situations past or present, is completely unintentional.

CHAPTER 1

Alice Maguire-Evans was *not* going into labor. She couldn't be! It was only mid-December, and the proverbial little bun was supposed to stay in the oven until early April. But the odd tightening sensation she kept feeling was disconcerting. And this was her first pregnancy. How was she supposed to know for sure what was normal and what wasn't?

"Everyone remain calm!" Alice's best friend, Owen James, was clearly *not* calm, but was attempting to give the impression that he was.

"We're taking you to Doc Howard right now." Alice's other best friend and sister-in-law Franny Brown-Maguire slung her brightly colored diaper bag over her shoulder and scooped up Theo, her seventeen-month old. With her free arm, she hefted his pop-up stroller, and headed for the back door.

They had all been visiting in the Paper Owl, Alice's bookshop, which sat right in the middle of Main Street in the tiny town of Blue Valley, Tennessee. Alice had been closing up shop while chatting with Owen and Franny. She'd just bent down to straighten a shelf display and when she'd stood up, the tightening sensation across her belly had begun.

Owen, who had read the pregnancy guidebook several times through, cover to cover, flew right into action. "We'll take my car," he said, jingling his keys. "It's Thursday evening and the festival kicks off tomorrow. Traffic could be an issue."

"Owen. Doc's clinic is like a block away," said Franny.

"Calm. Everyone stay calm," Owen reiterated.

Whereas Blue Valley was a tiny town most of the time, the population did swell quite a bit around high seasons and holidays. It would never be on par with the most popular tourist destinations in the state, because it was a good deal further off the beaten path, tucked away into a lovely little valley, the great Smoky Mountains standing guard all around it. But those who did manage to wind their way far enough along the twisting and turning roads that wove through the mountains and emerged above the sleepy valley, never regretted the journey, and always found a way to return. It was worth the trip and then some.

The town, which had grown up around its Main Street, boasted quiet, tree-lined lanes with cozy homes, a lovely park, a gorgeous lake, and enough quaint shops and restaurants to keep even the most discerning tourist happy for days. Especially when there was a special event going on—and *most* especially when that special event happened to be the Hometown Holidays Festival, which took place every December and lasted a whole week. This year, in fact, the planning committee, headed up by Alice herself, had decided to tack on a few extra days, kicking off on Friday and running all the way through Sunday of the following week. It would feature a 5k fun run, a Bavarian-style Christmas market, performances of the Dickens favorite, *A Christmas* Carol, food booths, wandering carolers, and even a faux ice skating rink in Town Park.

Owen was in the midst of struggling to open the door at the back of Alice's bookshop. It was cleverly disguised as just another bookshelf and led into the back hallway that ran along the entire historic building, which housed three establishments. Sourdough, Owen's bakery, was on one end, and Joe's, Franny's coffee shop, was on the other. The Paper Owl sat in between the two, and all three friends, along with their respective spouses, had apartments upstairs.

"I said, everyone remain calm!" Owen tried again with the door, finally throwing it open and ushering Alice through.

"Owen, we *are* calm," said Franny. "I'm sure everything will be fine," she assured Alice. "I had plenty of contractions like this when I was pregnant with Theo. But it won't hurt to have Doc Howard give you a quick once-over."

"Braxton Hicks contractions," said Owen, opening the door at the very back of the building which led out into the parking lot. "I've read all about them and I'm relatively sure that's what this is." He flung open the passenger-side door of his car, took Alice's hand, and helped her into the seat. "But we can't take any chances. Franny, you call Luke on the way to the clinic."

"No!" Alice put a hand on Owen's arm. Her husband, Detective Luke Evans, had been nervous enough about every little bout of heartburn or twinge of discomfort during this pregnancy. "Let's wait and see what Doc says first. Then I'll call Luke."

Luke, along with Alice's brother Ben—who was also Franny's husband—was up in Nashville for the weekend attending a law enforcement training event. Ben Maguire was the captain of the little local police force and Luke was head—and only—detective. Luckily, there was very little crime in Blue Valley, save the occasional larceny, burglary, or squirrels getting out of hand in someone's attic. Sure, now and then something of a more serious nature befell the little community, but thankfully, the streets of town were the kind that kids rode bicycles up and down and families strolled even after dark without hesitation. Ben and Luke would return on Sunday, and in the meantime, they'd left the trusty Officer Dewey and the newly-hired Officer Trimble in charge at the station.

They'd left Owen and Franny in charge of Alice.

Owen stabbed the key into the ignition, landing it in the keyhole on the third try and the engine roared to life. "Seatbelts!" he bellowed.

Franny, who had just snapped Theo into his car seat, reached up and patted Owen's shoulder from the backseat. "We're all buckled in. Nice and easy, now. There's no need to—"

But Owen had already squealed out of the parking lot and turned north onto Trout Lily Street, which ran behind the shops. He jerked to a stop and turned left on Phlox, honking at a pedestrian who'd made the mistake of putting a tentative foot out to cross the street.

"Owen!" Franny shrieked.

"Don't worry, Alice," Owen said. "We're almost there." They flew past the police station and the community center, crossed Main and passed St. Helena's Episcopal Church, screeching to a halt in front of Doc Howard's clinic at the corner of Phlox and Azalea, where Owen did a very bad job of fitting into a single parking space. He put the car in park, flung open his door, and ran around to help Alice out.

"Owen," said Alice, reaching over to turn off the ignition and pull out the key, "it might be a good idea to turn off the car before we go into the clinic." She handed him his keys and smiled. "I'm going to be fine." She put her hands over her belly as it tightened again. "Doc will know what to do."

Doc Howard, a true pillar of the community, had delivered half the population of Blue Valley. He was a rock—a salt-of-the-earth kind of person. His very presence was calming, and Alice had never seen him rattled by anything. His house was tucked in just behind his clinic, and both were located across the street from the Blue Valley hospital campus—a top notch facility for such a small town.

That was why it was so surprising to the friends

when they entered the clinic and found Doc leaning against the receptionist's desk, bent over with his hands on his knees, looking pale and badly shaken. As it was evening, the clinic was technically closed, and Doc was the only one there. Franny had called him on his cell phone when Alice's contractions had begun, so he'd walked over from his house especially to see her.

"Doc! What's happened?" Alice hurried up to him and put a hand on his back, momentarily forgetting her own worries. "Owen, get Doc some water."

Owen hurried and filled a cup from the dispenser in the corner.

Doc gratefully accepted the cup with trembling hands, took a sip, and set it on the desk. "I—I've just seen . . . a ghost!" He put a hand over his forehead and closed his eyes. "I know it sounds crazy, but it's true. I've just seen the ghost of my brother."

"Doc, I didn't even know you had a brother," said Owen, dragging two chairs over from the waiting area. "Sit. Both of you," he ordered, pointing back and forth between Alice and Doc.

"That's because he's been dead these last forty years," said Doc.

Both he and Alice sat down.

"Start from the beginning," said Alice.

Doc nodded and took a deep breath. "I got the call from Franny that you were on the way, so I was walking from the house to the clinic when I heard a noise coming from the backyard—sounded like it was coming from the old barn. A sort of scuttling sound. I figured it was those darn squirrels again. Anyway, I started to walk in that direction, and I swear I saw my brother Charles's face in the window. The light wasn't good, of course, with the sun just setting. But it was him!"

"What happened next?" asked Franny, tucking Theo into his stroller and handing him a sippy cup.

"I walked over there, opened the door, and—" Doc let out a long, slow breath. "No one was there." He shook his head and reached for the cup of water on the desk. "The cold front is blowing in, and the back door was banging in the wind. I swear I'd latched it last time I was out there." He looked into the cup, resting his elbows on his knees. "I'll never forget the day we got the call that Charles was dead. He lived in New York City. Terrible accident. His car veered off the road outside of town, hit a tree, and went up in flames. I never even—I never saw him again. So many things left unsaid." He sighed, then drank down the rest of the water. "He was only twenty-seven years old. A great scientist and doctor. Cut down before his prime."

Alice was glad to see the color returning to Doc's face. "Would it help if we all walk over together and check the barn right now?"

Doc shook his head. "I'm sure I just made a mistake. I saw something . . . but I don't know what it was. I'm playing the Ghost of Christmas Yet to Come in the play this year, you know. And it's forty years, almost to the day, since my brother died. I think my mind's just playing tricks on me." Doc seemed to shake off the incident. He stood. "Let's get you checked out, my dear. Oh—and let's not mention this to Mrs. Howard. No need to upset her."

After a quick exam, Doc was able to confirm that Alice was fine, the baby was fine, and there was no need to worry. Alice's pregnancy was moving along just as it should. Doc advised her to drink plenty of water, rest when she needed to, and not to stress too much about the holiday festival. He walked the group to the door.

"Don't worry, Doc," said Owen. "We'll keep our eyes open. If there's a ghost in your barn, we'll scare it away."

Doc laughed and shook his head, fully back to his

CHAPTER 2

The Hometown Holidays Festival got underway the following afternoon, right on schedule. Alice hefted her giant red three-ring binder onto the counter at the bookshop. She'd sat at the helm of this event long enough that she had memorized every tab, every section and subsection in the notebook. She referenced the front pages, which she'd laminated. These ten pages showed detailed schedules on the fronts and lists of volunteers and supplies on the backs—one page for each day of the festival.

Alice ran a finger down the first page. "Morning setup, check. Lunch with the Main Street shopkeepers, check. Mayor Abercrombie's welcome at the Town Park gazebo, check . . ." Alice felt such satisfaction when she checked things off any given to-do list.

She was interrupted by the bells above the shop door jingling. Pearl Ann and Norman McKenzie, who were dear friends of Alice, came in.

"A funny thing just happened," Pearl Ann said, coming to the counter and eyeing the giant red binder. "I had three different customers cancel appointments at the spa this afternoon, and I find I have extra time on my hands."

Pearl Ann owned Blue Beauty, a spa just across Main Street and a few doors down. Her husband, Norman, owned Odd Job Bob, a handyman business. He stepped up to the counter next.

"And what's even crazier is that I also had my afternoon job cancelled. Isn't that strange?"

Alice raised a brow, looking back and forth between them. "That is . . . unusual, as booked as you two normally are. What are you going to do with all the unexpected free time?"

"That's why we're here!" said Pearl Ann, slapping a hand on the counter. "We don't know what to do with ourselves and were hoping you had a job or two for us—you know, to help out with the festival." She nodded at the binder.

"Oh! Well . . . are you sure?"

Both Pearl Ann and Norman nodded enthusiastically. It wasn't until Alice had sent the two out with their assignments—to check the supply of commemorative festival mugs at the Smiling Hound Pub across the street, and to go down to the park to meet the faux ice rink company, Nice Ice, to show them where to set up the rink—that she realized that Owen and Franny had probably put Pearl Ann and Norman up to the sudden urge to volunteer their time so generously.

"That was very nice of you," she told Owen when he came in through the bookcase door.

"What?"

"You too," Alice said to Franny, as she came in through the large, cased opening that separated the Paper Owl from Joe's.

"Whatever do you mean?" asked Franny, grinning.

"You two put Pearl Ann and Norman up to cancelling their afternoon appointments so they could help out with the festival," said Alice. "But remember, Doc says I'm fine. You didn't have to do that."

Franny and Owen looked at each other, then back at Alice.

"What are you talking about?" asked Owen.

"Don't act like you don't know," said Alice.

"Okay," said Owen with a shrug. "I'm always happy to take credit for nice things I didn't do."

"Well, I'm off to Sugarbuzz to talk to Doug and Barb," said Alice, shutting the binder and shoving it into her backpack.

"About this year's chocolate fountain?" asked Owen. "Already did that. They're all set and ready to go."

"Seriously?" Alice stopped and turned to look at him. "And what about the—"

"Fondu dippers?" said Franny. "All taken care of. We'll have a vast array of goodies to dip into the chocolate this year. Cookies, fruit, marshmallows, those tiny donuts everyone loves . . ."

"Oh," said Alice, pausing. "Thanks." She tucked her backpack behind the counter and hung her coat on one of the pegs on the wall. "Well then, I guess I'll . . ."

"Have a nice cup of tea?" said Franny, disappearing into Joe's and returning with a steaming mug of Alice's favorite ginger-raspberry tea. "Extra honey," she added with a smile.

Alice thanked Franny, took a sip, savoring the sweet warmth, and sat down on the stool behind the counter. "I guess that frees me up to talk with you about tomorrow's Holiday Cookie Exchange," she said, looking at Owen over the rim of her mug.

"It's going to go off without a hitch," Owen assured her.

Back before Thanksgiving, he and Alice's mom, Bea Maguire, had decided to do a family holiday cookie exchange, where each guest brought a few dozen of their favorite cookie along with enough copies of the recipe for everyone. By the time the party was over, every guest would have a full supply of cookies to serve through the holidays, plus a fistful of recipes so that they could bake their favorites at home.

Originally, it was going to be a small family affair —just the Maguires, Franny's parents the Browns, and Owen. Owen's husband, Michael, wouldn't be able to attend as he always visited his family before Christmas. Michael, who was head concierge at the luxury mountain resort in town as well as a gifted poet, had made Owen promise to bring along his vanilla pizzelles, which were thin, crisp cookies made by pouring batter into a specially designed iron which pressed beautiful images into the surfaces. The recipe had been handed down in Michael's family for generations, and he made a big batch every Christmas and served them with hot cups of sweet amaretto coffee for dipping.

Well, what had started out to be a small family party had grown. A few close friends said they'd love to participate, then a few of those friends' friends joined in, and finally, Bea and Owen had decided to take the Hometown Holidays Festival by storm and add the cookie exchange as an official event. Now, visitors from all over had registered to come, each of them bringing huge batches of their own pride-and-joy recipes.

"Maybe now that I suddenly have all of this free time on my hands, I should come up with a stellar cookie recipe for the exchange," said Alice.

Owen gave a little snort and patted her on the shoulder. "Or you could just take it easy and let me do the baking."

"Are you saying I'm not a good baker? That I can't produce a respectable cookie?"

"No, no! Not at all! It's just, Doc did say you shouldn't stress too much."

Before Alice could remind him once again that she was fine and didn't want to be coddled too much, the bells above the door jingled and Mrs. Howard, Doc's wife, came in.

"Hello all!" she said. "Owen, Hilda told me you

were here. I've come to talk about the centerpieces for the cookie exchange."

Mrs. Howard—who was everyone's favorite English teacher at Blue Valley High, and quite the cookie afficionado herself—was the third member of Owen and Bea's planning team. And Hilda Becker was Owen's assistant at the bakery.

"Wonderful," said Owen. "Let's go have a cup of coffee at Joe's. We can draw out a diagram. I want people to be able to sample cookies and gather recipes without any bottlenecks."

"By the way, Mrs. H," said Franny, "Have you happened to notice anything odd going on around your barn?"

Alice shot Franny a look.

"The barn in my backyard?" Mrs. Howard pursed her lips thoughtfully. "No, Franny, I can't say that I have. Why do you ask?"

"No reason," said Franny. "That cold front blew in and I noticed some of the older structures around town got a little beaten up."

"How old is that barn, anyway?" asked Owen.

"Oh, I'd say over a hundred fifty years old. You know, the house Doc and I live in was his house as a boy. We renovated it, of course, after we married. But he and his brother used to play in that barn, and I imagine his father before him did, too. Doc's grandfather built it. Of course, it's needed to be stabilized and updated a bit through the years—a coat of paint here, a support beam there. Otherwise, it might not have fared so well. But for the most part, it's very well made."

"They don't make them like they used to," said Owen with a sigh.

As he and Mrs. Howard headed toward the cased opening, Mrs. Howard's cell phone rang. She stopped to answer, saying only a few words, her face turning pale and her hand dropping to her side as soon as she'd ended the call.

"Mrs. H, what is it?" asked Alice, hurrying over to the woman. Something was most definitely wrong, judging by the deep lines that creased her face.

"It's Doc," said Mrs. Howard, putting a hand to her heart. "He's been taken to the emergency room. He collapsed."

CHAPTER 3

Dusk was just beginning to settle over town, and twinkling holiday lights were setting off draped garlands and light posts as everyone stepped out onto Main Street. Franny gave her parents a quick call to check on Theo, who was still on his grandparent play-date in the park with the Maguires and the Browns. When Franny told them she might be a bit late to pick him up, they all gladly offered to take Theo out for dinner at the Smiling Hound, telling Franny not to worry about a thing.

"It's so kind of you all to go with me to the hospital," said Mrs. Howard, who was still shaken, but had taken a few deep breaths and regained her high school English teacher take-charge attitude. After driving in Owen's car to Doc Howard's the night before, they'd quickly decided it would be faster to walk to the hospital and were already making the turn from Main onto Phlox. "I just can't imagine what happened to Doc." She glanced at Alice. "You saw him just last night—I remember him walking over to the clinic from the house when you all came by. Did he seem okay to you then?"

Alice caught Owen's eyes, then Franny's. "He was fine," she assured Mrs. Howard.

"He seemed a little off when he returned home after your appointment, but he was perfectly fine this morning before he left for work, and also when I saw him at lunchtime," Mrs. Howard reasoned. "Maybe he collapsed because of a dip in blood sugar. Or dehydration. Sometimes he gets so busy he forgets to keep up with his water."

"I'll bet that's it," said Franny.

"I'll feel better once I've seen him," said Mrs. Howard. She walked resolutely up the steps at the hospital's front entrance and pushed the large glass door open.

But she didn't feel better when she saw him. No one did. They'd been directed to room 258, down at the end of the hall in the patient tower of the hospital, and had opened the door to find Doc, looking pale and wan, sound asleep in his bed, an IV attached to his right arm.

"Oh, my dear!" said Mrs. Howard, hurrying over to her husband's side and bending near.

Doc roused a bit, tried to focus on his wife's face, offered a tiny smile, and fell back into what appeared to be a somewhat fitful sleep. He twitched around, mumbling incoherently. A nurse popped her head into the room.

"Hello, Mrs. Howard," she said, coming inside.

"Oh, hello Sally." Mrs. Howard waved a hand around. "Everyone, you all know Sally Sanderson, don't you?"

They all nodded. In a town as small as Blue Valley, everyone pretty much knew everyone else, at least a little bit. Alice knew that Sally was a seasoned nurse, and had gotten to know her better recently when she'd stopped by the hospital to sign up for the *Bringing Baby Home: Don't Panic! You Can Do This!* class that was coming up in a few months.

"I'll go tell Dr. McCorkle you're here," said Sally, giving a quick glance at Doc's IV drip and tucking his blanket around his shoulder.

When Sally left, the sound of the door closing behind her must've roused Doc, because he suddenly opened his eyes wide, and sat bolt upright in bed. "I saw him! Charles!"

Mrs. Howard quickly took hold of her husband's hand. "I'm right here, my darling," she said. "You're okay. You're in the hospital."

Doc turned shaken eyes to her. "I saw him. My brother. The ghost of Charles."

"You—I think you were dreaming."

He solemnly shook his head. "I should've told you. Last night, in barn." He seemed to notice for the first time that Alice, Owen, and Franny were standing with his wife. "It's okay. You can tell her now," he said, then flopped back onto the pillows, his eyes closed.

Mrs. Howard frowned and turned to the others. "Tell me what? What is he talking about?"

Just then, the door opened, and Nurse Sally came back in, this time with a serious looking woman in a white coat with a stethoscope draped around her neck and a clipboard in her hand.

"Dr. McCorkle," Mrs. Howard said, her shoulders dropping in relief. "Please tell me you know what's going on with Doc."

"We're getting to the bottom of it," the doctor assured her. "I've already alerted the police."

"The police?" Mrs. Howard's hands flew to her mouth. "What for?"

Dr. McCorkle tucked the clipboard under her arm. "Mrs. Howard, we believe your husband has ingested some kind of poison. Now, there's certainly a chance that this was simply accidental. However, in cases such as this, we must be absolutely sure that there has been no foul play. I'm waiting on some lab results to pinpoint the substance. I'll know better then how to treat it. For now, he's recovering from having his stomach pumped. He's receiving fluids, nutrients, and medication to help with the pain." She pointed her pen at the IV bag.

"He just told me he saw the ghost of his brother," said Mrs. Howard.

Dr. McCorkle's lips tightened into a thin line. "Charles?"

Owen nudged Alice with his elbow.

"Oh yes—I forgot you and Charles were in the same graduating class in high school," said Mrs. Howard.

"He's been dead for years now, hasn't he?" The doctor's face softened a tiny bit, but then she went right back to being all business. "I'm sure your husband's vision of his brother came on as a result of the pain medication he's on. It's not at all uncommon for such things to occur."

Mrs. Howard breathed a sigh of relief. "Oh. Of course. Thank goodness."

"Don't listen to her, dear," Doc mumbled almost incoherently from the bed. "She *hated* Charles."

All eyes in the room turned to Dr. McCorkle, who had a deep crease between her brows. She shook her head. "Nonsense. Like I said, he's really medicated for now, to keep him comfortable and to help him rest. But the good news is, he's hopefully on the mend and will be fine. I think I'll very likely discharge him tomorrow to continue to recuperate at home."

With a nod, the doctor left the room, followed by Sally, just as Officer Dewey entered.

Dewey smiled down at the now-sleeping Doc. "I hear he's going to be just fine," he said.

"Thank heaven," said Mrs. Howard. She glanced at Doc, then stepped closer to Dewey and lowered her voice. "The doctor said he'd been poisoned?"

"That's what I'm here to talk to you about, ma'am," said Dewey. "I wanted you to know I've got Officer Trimble over at Doc's office right now. I came to the hospital to talk to Dr. McCorkle. My understanding is that Doc had been seeing patients as per usual all day. Harriet said he was feeling just fine as far as she could tell. He'd gone back to his office to fill out some paperwork, and Harriet put a call through to him . . ." Dewey shook his head. "When he didn't answer, she went running in there and found him on the floor. At first she thought he'd had a heart attack or something of that nature. She called for an ambulance, and of course, being as the hospital was right across the street, it didn't take them long to get him in and start eliminating the possible causes. Dr. McCorkle called us when she suspected poison or some kind of drug. Said his lips were turning blue and his pupils were dilated, plus his blood pressure was all over the place. Thank goodness they got whatever it was out of his stomach before he absorbed too much of it."

Poor Mrs. Howard was trembling by this time. "Who would do such a thing to Doc? Everyone loves him!"

The police radio on Dewey's shoulder came to life, the voice of young Officer Trimble, the new hire at the station, coming over the line. "Officer Dewey? You there? Over."

Dewey held up a finger and took the radio out of its holster. "Right here, Trimble. What've you got?"

"I think I might've found the culprit. I'll send you a snapshot over your cell. Doc was eating them shortly before he collapsed."

The cell phone at Dewey's hip dinged and he took

it out and looked at it, frowning. He looked at Mrs. Howard. "Do these look familiar, ma'am?"

Everyone peered at the photograph—a tin of red and white striped cookies in the shapes of candy canes.

"Those look delicious," said Owen.

"I've seen those before!" said Mrs. Howard. "I stopped by the office for lunch today—I always have lunch with Doc during school holidays. Harriet had Christmas gifts on her desk, all for Doc from his patients, including that tin of cookies. I even teased him about them—told him not to eat any until his afternoon snack time."

"Any idea who sent the cookies?" asked Dewey.

"No," said Mrs. Howard, shaking her head sadly. "They were so pretty I asked. Harriet said they were sitting on top of the morning paper outside the door when she arrived this morning. People always bring in gifts and treats for Doc at Christmas, so it wasn't unusual. I can't believe this is happening!"

A loud snore came from the direction of the bed, and everyone looked back at Doc.

"He seems more peaceful now," said Alice. "Thank goodness he's going to be okay." She patted her belly. "He has a baby to deliver in a few months!"

Mrs. Howard smiled. "And he wouldn't miss that

for the world. You know, this business with thinking he's seen the ghost of his brother Charles . . . I've been thinking about that. Doc is playing the Ghost of Christmas Yet to Come in the play down at the community center. And his brother died all those years ago, during the Christmas season. I think in his delirious state, with the medication and all, he's probably just mixing those things up somewhere in his mind."

"Doc said as much himself," said Owen.

Mrs. Howard pulled a chair over to Doc's bedside and took a seat. Nurse Sally came back in and offered coffee or soda, and Mrs. Howard accepted the coffee. Alice, Owen, and Franny, satisfied that Doc would be resting and recovering overnight, said their goodbyes and headed out of the hospital along with Dewey.

"Who could've given Doc those cookies?" Franny wondered, pulling her sweater tighter around herself. The wind had whipped up considerably since they'd gone into the hospital earlier. Now, they had to raise their voices just to hear one another over its howling.

"Good question," said Alice, who had gotten used to being hot during her pregnancy and was rather enjoying the chilly wind blowing through her hair. "I mean, everyone loves Doc."

"We'll try to figure that out, but Trimble says

there are no fingerprints on the tin," said Dewey.

They were walking along Azalea Street before turning onto Phlox, just passing the Howards' house.

Alice stopped and looked at the house, now dark and shadowy in the glow of the flickering street lights. "Something's bothering me, and I didn't want to say it to Mrs. Howard now when she's finally feeling a little better about this whole situation." She looked at Dewey. "Last night at my appointment with Doc, he told us all he'd just seen the ghost of his brother. And that was before he received those cookies."

Dewey frowned. "So, these visions of the ghost had nothing to do with whatever was in the cookies, or with the medication Doc's receiving at the hospital."

Alice shook her head slowly.

"Hey, don't look now," said Owen, tapping Dewey on the shoulder. Owen swallowed and pointed. "But there's a ghost in Doc's barn."

CHAPTER 4

Before she knew what was happening, Alice found herself being hustled into a large clump of bushes in the garden bed at the side of the Howards' house.

"Hurry!" hissed Owen. "We can't let the ghost— or whoever's in there—see us!"

"This is nuts," whispered Dewey. "I'm an officer of the law. I should just walk into that barn and confront the . . . the . . ." He pushed a branch aside and peered at the barn. "What the heck is that?"

Owen moved a branch aside to get a better view, and everyone else followed suit.

A light seemed to be moving around inside the barn, as though someone was searching for something. Then, for a brief moment, a pale face moved into the frame of the window to the side of the large front door, but then was gone.

"I'm screaming on the inside," said Owen.

"Me too," said Dewey. He cleared his throat. "Uh, I mean—"

There was a sudden banging sound from inside the barn. Then it happened again. And again.

"What was that?" Alice whispered, grabbing Owen's arm.

Owen gasped. "Oh my gosh, Alice. Release your death grip!"

"I think I can hear . . . voices?" Alice strained to hear the sounds emanating from the barn, but they were hard to make out with the whistling of the wind in her ears and in the branches of their obliging bushy hideout.

"We could see better if we moved in a little bit closer," Dewey suggested. "Look, just follow the chain of bushes. That way."

They all moved, staying close together, through the bushes, which wound in a leafy line toward the barn. Then they crouched down and waited. There was another slam.

"I'm going in there," said Dewey, standing.

"I'll go with you," whimpered Owen.

Everyone moved silently toward the barn, Dewey in the lead.

Owen linked arms with Alice and Franny, creeping forward, all the while whispering, "It's just squirrels. It's just squirrels. It's just—"

They all froze at the sight of a shadowy figure running from the back side of the barn, its long, white hair flying behind.

This time Owen let out a blood-curdling scream that could've been heard all the way over on Main Street were it not for the gusting wind.

"Okay, I'm officially scared now," said Franny. "Who, or *what*, was that?"

Dewey forged ahead now, taking off in the direction the apparition had run, but returning a few moments later, panting. "They got away," he said, leading the way into the barn. The back door was opening and closing in the wind, slamming into the side of the building, accounting for the banging sound they'd heard before.

A flashlight lay on the floor, still turned on, casting a fan of light in the otherwise darkened room.

"Don't touch anything," Dewey warned, flipping on his own flashlight, and scanning the barn's interior.

Alice took inventory as the shadowy shapes in the

room were illuminated, one by one. "Bales of hay . . . a stack of old lumber . . . a mop and bucket—"

"I thought that was a skeleton," said Owen, relieved.

"Hold on. Shine the light over there again, by those boxes," said Alice, pointing toward the stack of boxes Dewey had just passed over. "Lower."

Dewey lowered the beam of light to the base of the bottom box and scanned.

Alice sucked in a breath. "A hand." Her voice quavered. "Over there . . . to the left . . ."

"What?" Dewey stilled the light and moved it back.

"A hand! It's a hand. A human hand," said Alice, pointing with a trembling finger.

The beam of light caught on what was, indeed, a human hand, palm-up and sticking out from behind the boxes.

"Stay here," Dewey ordered, and walked over and around the stack.

Of course, no one followed his order. Instead, they followed Dewey, and thus all saw it at once—the prone form of a man, lying face down, very still on the floor. Dewey quickly knelt next to him and felt for a pulse. Then he let out a shallow sigh and stood. "He's dead."

CHAPTER 5

What followed was a bit of a blur to Alice. Dewey had carefully turned the dead man over to reveal the obvious cause of death—a knife, plunged into his chest in the region of his heart. Blood had spread from the wound and was smeared all over the floor. Alice had almost fainted at the sight, but thankfully had been supported by her friends, who took her outside, where they all sat huddled together on a garden bench that was sheltered by a little alcove in the Howards' backyard between the house and the barn.

Unfortunately, they'd all seen murder victims before. The trio of friends, in fact, had a penchant for mystery solving, a natural tendency to obstinately butt in even when ordered not to, and a collective sense of curiosity that increased exponentially when they were in each other's company and in the presence of unanswered questions. These qualities had led them to be of assistance to the police on numerous occasions—even though the police still vigilantly insisted that they keep their distance.

Officer Trimble arrived within minutes—in part because Doc's house was such a short distance from the police station, where he'd been on call. Dewey went out and searched the trees the white-haired phantom had disappeared into but found nothing. An ambulance sped across the street from the hospital and the EMTs kindly tucked blankets around Alice, Owen, and Franny before carrying their stretcher inside the barn where they would wait to move the body until the police gave the go-ahead.

Alice's cell phone buzzed, and she answered the call. She had never been happier to hear her husband's voice.

"Dewey filled us in on what happened," said Luke. "We're going to get home as quickly as we can, but the weather here is awful. Are you okay?"

"I'm fine. Just . . . a little shaken."

"Are you sure? Is the baby okay?"

"We're fine," Alice assured him.

She'd heard on the news that afternoon about the

arctic front that had blasted down from the north and had passed through Nashville bringing with it record-breaking lows—unfortunately following on the heels of thunderstorms. That combination had made for dangerous, icy road conditions and if the predictions were right, more rain was on the way—rain that would freeze overnight. Alice had been grateful that Luke and Ben wouldn't need to get on the road for home until Sunday, by which time the weather should have improved.

"Oh, Alice, I wish I was there with you right now."

Alice could hear the desperation in Luke's voice. But she didn't want him taking any foolish chances trying to drive under the circumstances.

"Me too," she said. "But Dewey and Trimble are very capable officers."

Dewey had also called on a couple of other off-duty officers, and they were all pooling their investigative resources and carefully picking apart the crime scene. They'd brought in several spotlights, as the overhead lights in the old barn didn't do much to illuminate the area. They were busy taking photos and looking for clues while Alice, Owen, and Franny waited to make their statements so that they could go home.

Alice and Luke talked for a few minutes more—Luke promising to come home as soon as the roads were safe, and Alice insisting that she was fine.

"I wish Luke and Ben were here," said Franny, clicking off her cell phone after talking to Ben.

"And Michael," said Owen, clicking off his after talking to his husband.

"I need a piece of pie," said Alice, feeling her stomach growl.

Dewey came outside then and went over the events of the evening one more time, as well as having Alice, Owen, and Franny reiterate exactly what Doc had said he'd seen in his barn the night before.

"You three need to go on home," said Dewey, tucking his notebook into his pocket. "I'll get in touch if I have any more questions."

"Have you called the Howards?" asked Alice.

"Yes. Doc is finally sleeping more soundly, and Mrs. Howard is planning to stay overnight at the hospital." He nodded toward the ambulance. "As soon as the guys get back over there with the body, I'll have to have her take a look to see if she can ID the guy."

"So, you don't know who it is?" asked Franny.

"Never seen him before," said Dewey, shaking his head.

Officer Trimble came out of the barn and called him over, so he gave them all a nod and said he'd see them later. He and Trimble went over to the ambulance, where they conferred quietly with the EMTs. Meanwhile, Alice, Owen, and Franny should've been in a hurry to pick up Theo and get home. It was chilly and dark, and none of them had eaten dinner yet. But instead, they looked at one another, made an unspoken agreement, and walked quietly and briskly back over to the barn, where they peered inside.

The body still lay there where it had been before, but looked more gruesome now, the pale skin and sticky blood more clearly visible in the bright lights.

"This is just awful," said Franny.

"And bizarre," said Owen. When Alice and Franny looked at him, he added, "The dead guy looks exactly like Doc Howard."

CHAPTER 6

"I'll get the coffee," said Franny with a yawn the next morning.

The three friends had stayed up half the night after leaving the Howards' house. They'd all been so spooked that they'd piled into Alice's little living room, where they'd stayed up late watching comforting movies they'd seen a million times before. They'd tucked Theo into his little portable crib, and Owen had brought his and Michael's pride and joy—their Yorkshire terrier puppy, Franklin—over along with his puppy bed and a selection of treats and toys. Franklin got along very well with Alice and Luke's dog Finn, as well as their calico cat, Poppy, and the three animals seemed to consider the whole slumber party to be one big playdate.

Saturday morning, it was Theo who woke first, refreshed and ready to play and delighted to find himself in Aunt Alice and Uncle Luke's living room. This suited the pets just fine, and soon baby giggles and the clicking of puppy paws on the wood floor roused the slumbering grownups, who had a harder time shaking off their sleepiness. Still, as it was almost time to open up shop downstairs, everyone yawned and stretched, and headed out to the rooftop garden for some fresh air.

The sun was just making its way over the mountaintops on the east end of the valley, and the sky was beginning to lighten when Franny returned to the garden, bringing a couple of carafes of coffee and Officer Dewey along with her, who carried enough mugs for everyone. As was often the case, Dewey had come into Joe's with the early morning crowd.

After Theo's birth, Franny had begun to have her faithful assistant manager, Beth, take the earliest shift, affording Franny a bit more time to get herself up and ready and to transport Theo to whichever set of grandparents would be watching him that day. She and Ben had visited the new local daycare center and preschool, Little Sprouts—which was catacorner from the Maguires' house by the park—but the grandparents wouldn't hear of them putting Theo in daycare until he was a bit older . . . if ever. Alice wondered if they'd change their tune once they had *two* active grandkids.

"I asked Franny if I could come up for a quick chat," said Dewey, as Franny poured coffee all around. "I thought I'd better tell you what happened after you left last night."

"Oh no. Are the Howards okay?" asked Alice.

"Oh yes, they're fine. Doc's getting better by the hour," Dewey said quickly. He paused and looked down into his coffee mug. "The Howards are going to need all the support and encouragement they can get over the next few days and weeks."

"They must be relieved that whoever the man was who was prowling around in their barn is no longer a threat, at least," said Alice, sitting down at the little café table and filling her lungs with the cold, fresh morning air in an attempt to compensate for the lack of caffeine in her coffee.

"Although they're probably *not* too relieved that some knife-toting silver-haired creature killed him," added Owen.

"I'm afraid . . ." Dewey paused. "I'm afraid the last thing they feel is relief." He cleared his throat. "You told me that Doc thought he'd seen the ghost of his brother out in the barn on Thursday night. Well . . . turns out it *was* his brother."

"But—" Owen sloshed his coffee, burning his hand and causing him to drop his mug which shattered on the ground. Theo gave a rousing round of applause from his highchair. "Doc's brother has been dead for ages!"

"Turns out he wasn't," said Dewey.

"How could that be? Did they bury someone other than the brother?" asked Alice.

"They didn't bury anybody, remember?" said Franny. "Or at least that was my impression. Doc said the car accident and the fire were so awful that there wasn't much of anything left inside."

"There were human remains after that accident such as they were," said Dewey. "But no DNA tests were run on them because it was definitely Charles Howard's car. Plus, his class ring from medical school, engraved with his name and the date he graduated, was found with the, er, what was left of the body. There was no reason to suspect it was anyone else because Charles Howard was unaccounted for from that time forward. They did bury those remains.

"Last night, when the body was brought into the hospital morgue, Mrs. Howard took a quick look and almost passed out on the spot because the dead man looked so much like Doc. Later, Doc woke up, found out about it, and insisted on being wheeled down-stairs. He took one look and knew instantly that it was his older brother, even though they hadn't seen each other in so many years. Said he had the Howard chin, that he looked just like their dad." He sighed. "It hit him pretty hard, I can tell you."

"He must be devastated. He's got to grieve his brother all over again," said Franny. She pulled Theo out of his highchair and held him close.

Dewey nodded. "We're looking into the mystery of how all of this happened, of course." He sighed. "Meanwhile, like I said, the Howards can use all our support."

"We'll run over there this morning," said Owen, tossing the last of his broken coffee mug into a bin.

"You'll find Mrs. H at home," said Dewey, setting his empty mug on the table. "She was going to get a shower and a change of clothes before heading back over to the hospital."

"Good. Since it's Saturday, we've all got plenty of help down in our shops," said Alice. "We'll get a few things done and then go right over."

Dewey nodded and started to walk through the garden toward the French doors that led into Alice's living room. He stopped and turned back. "I know

CHAPTER 7

Once Alice had opened the Paper Owl, given her part-time employees Lacie and Zack instructions for the morning, and checked over the daily festival schedule and to-do list in her giant red binder, she grabbed her bag and went through the cased opening into Joe's, where Owen and Franny were already waiting. Owen buckled Theo into his stroller, and they all walked first to the Maguires' house to drop him off, then over to Phlox Street by way of Trout Lily, enjoying the quaint houses all draped in wreaths and garlands along the way. As it was Saturday, the Hometown Holidays Festival would soon be in full swing, and early bird tourists were already strolling along Main Street, looking for breakfast before the days' events began.

As it turned out, they were not the first visitors of the day to arrive at the Howards' house. Father Amos from St. Helena's was just leaving, along with the church organist, Myrtle Bodkins. They stopped when they saw Alice and volunteered on the spot to help out at the big cookie exchange later that day, and to get others in the parish family to step up and do whatever Alice needed in the week to come as the festival continued. Pearl Ann and Norman McKenzie, who'd been chatting with Mrs. Howard, walked inside with a casserole dish covered in tinfoil. When they came back outside, they told Alice they'd be glad to lend a hand over at the ice skating rink in the park once they got off work.

Mrs. Howard herself was standing out on the front porch, visiting with Annabelle Swift, a fellow teacher from the high school. Mrs. Swift was Mrs. Howard's equivalent in experience—but where Mrs. Howard headed up the team of English teachers, Mrs. Swift was the cornerstone of the math department. Alice had a momentary pang of panic on seeing Mrs. Swift, as she had been her teacher for both Algebra I and Algebra II, neither of which had been Alice's best subjects.

"These cookies look divine," Mrs. Howard was just saying.

Annabelle sniffled, dabbing at her eyes with a wadded up tissue. "It's the least I could do. And I'm so glad Doc is on the mend and will be home soon."

"As am I," said Mrs. Howard, putting a hand on Annabelle's shoulder and giving her a look of sympathy. "I plan to spoil him rotten and try to force him to rest—although knowing my husband, that might not be possible." She chuckled, then turned more serious. "Annabelle, I am sorry about Charles, for your sake as well as my husband's. I know you must have mixed emotions about his death."

Annabelle nodded. "It had been so long since I'd seen him or heard anything about him. But even so, it's never easy to lose . . . someone who was . . . once very dear."

Alice, Owen, and Franny stood politely to the side, not wanting to interrupt the conversation. After a few more quiet words between the two women, as well as a hug, Annabelle said goodbye and walked down the porch steps, giving the three friends a nod as she passed them.

"She never did like me," Alice whispered to Franny.

"She knew you didn't like math," Mrs. Howard said from the porch, raising a brow at Alice.

"Looks like you won't have to think of what to

cook for dinner tonight," said Owen, putting an arm around Mrs. Howard and leading her back into the house.

"Or for the next few weeks. Look at all this food!" She set Annabelle's cookies on the counter in her sunny kitchen. There was quite an array of foil-covered dishes, and the smell of home cooking filled the air. "Pearl Ann brought that wonderful mushroom chicken pasta casserole she makes."

"Ooh, I love that one," said Franny.

Alice's stomach growled.

"And Marge Hartfield brought over a loaf of French bread and a salad to go with it," Mrs. Howard continued. "The Whitmans brought enough potato salad to feed an army."

Marge owned the Waxy Wick, the candle shop across the street from the Paper Owl, and the Whitmans owned and operated Whitman's Market.

Mrs. Howard looked through the window at the kitchen sink, down the front walk in the direction Annabelle had gone. "And of course, dear Annabelle brought dessert. Doc and I are so very blessed."

"It sounded like Annabelle was a friend of Doc's brother," said Alice.

Mrs. Howard nodded. "Way back in high school. They were sweethearts—actually got engaged." She sighed. "But Annabelle changed her mind and broke it off. Broke poor Charles's heart. I think she's always felt guilty over that, even though it has long since been water under the bridge."

They put the food into the refrigerator and walked back through the living room toward the front porch.

"When do you expect Doc to be released?" asked Owen, holding the door open and letting the ladies pass through.

"Tonight, if we're lucky," said Mrs. Howard. "It helps that we live right across the street from the hospital. I think Samantha will be satisfied that he can rest just as easily at home as he can in that bed."

"Samantha? Oh—you mean Dr. McCorkle?" asked Alice. "Didn't you say that she and Doc's brother were also in the same class back in high school?"

"And that reminds me: didn't Doc say Dr. McCorkle always hated his brother?" added Owen.

"He did mumble something about that . . ." Mrs. Howard put her hands on the porch railing and frowned. "You know, even though Charles was only a few years older, I never really knew him. He always seemed like this busy, important, far-away person . . . and then he moved to New York soon after he graduated medical school. And of course, then he died . . .

or so we thought." She shook her head. "All those years he and Doc might've been close. Lost." She gave a small shrug. "I hope at some point we come to a clearer understanding of why Charles did what he did."

"Dewey says they'll figure it out," Franny assured her.

Just then, the downtown postal carrier, Henry Witherspoon, came trotting up the walk whistling a Christmas tune, his mail bag slung over his shoulder and a sprig of holly sticking out from his hat.

"I have a few cards and letters for you and Doc today," he said cheerfully, digging through the bag. He handed Mrs. Howard a small stack of mail. "Tell Doc we're all thinking of him."

"Thank you, Henry. I will," said Mrs. Howard. She glanced down at the envelopes in her hand. "I'll take these cards to Doc in the hospital. I'm sure they'll cheer him right up."

Henry gave them a little salute and headed off to his next stop.

"Let us walk with you across the street," said Owen, offering his arm to Mrs. Howard.

"We'd love to check in on Doc," added Alice.

"That would be lovely," said Mrs. Howard. She

tucked the mail into her purse and took Owen's arm, and they all crossed the street together.

As they were approaching the hospital entrance, Officer Dewey jogged up behind them. "I was just coming over to talk with you," he said to Mrs. Howard.

"Good morning, Gannon," said Mrs. Howard in her practiced English teacher voice.

Dewey whipped off his hat. "Good morning, Mrs. Howard."

"*Gannon*?" Owen whispered. "Dewey's first name is *Gannon*?"

Alice and Franny simultaneously elbowed him.

"We got our test results back and confirmed what Dr. Swift already suspected. Doc had consumed a fair amount of tetrahydrozoline—and the same drug was found on those candy cane cookies."

"Tetra-what?" said Owen.

"The stuff in eyedrops?" asked Franny. When all heads turned her direction, she added, "I'm the mother of a toddler. I'm sleep deprived. I go through gallons of the stuff."

"Yes, Franny," Dewey confirmed. "That is exactly what tetrahydrozoline is."

Mrs. Howard put her hands on her hips. "So,

someone tried to kill my darling husband with *eyedrops*?"

"Not necessarily," said Dewey. "We're more of the mind that someone tried to make Doc sick. And succeeded. Dr. McCorkle said he had an unusually sensitive reaction. But then, on the other hand, if he'd eaten too many more of those cookies . . ."

"It could've killed him?" Mrs. Howard put a hand to her heart.

Owen gasped. "Do we think this was the same someone who killed Doc's brother?"

"As to whether it's the same culprit . . . it could be," Dewey continued. "Maybe someone had a beef with both the Howard brothers. We just don't know yet." He shoved his hands into his pockets. "At this point, what happened to Doc could've been anything from attempted murder to an ill-conceived prank."

"It seems awfully coincidental that both brothers would be attacked one after the other," reasoned Mrs. Howard.

"I agree," said Dewey. He gave Alice, Owen, and Franny a pointed look, then gently took Mrs. Howard's arm. "Mrs. H, I need to speak to you about something else. You and Doc are about to receive a visitor. Uh—" He looked at the others again, and then pulled Mrs. Howard aside.

"We read you loud and clear, *Gannon*," said Owen, opening the door to the hospital lobby. "We'll see you upstairs, Mrs. H."

They stepped off the elevator on the second floor and went straight down the hall to Doc's room. Alice peeped in first, saw that Doc was awake, and signaled the others.

"Come in, come in," Doc said with a warm smile. He was sitting up in bed, eating a cup of red Jell-O. "How are you feeling today, Alice? Any more of those contractions?"

"A few," Alice admitted. "I'm glad I know they're normal, thanks to you. But more importantly, how are you?"

"Much better. I haven't slept this much in the last twenty-five years put together! I'm hoping they'll let me out of here later today. All I'm doing is laying around, and I can do that in my own bed at home." He shook his head. "This has been a crazy few days."

"We're so sorry about your brother," Franny said.

Doc looked down at his Jell-o. "So am I," he said sadly. "All this time . . ." He shook off the thought. "Well. It doesn't do any good to dwell on everything I regret."

"Doc, do you have any idea who would want to

hurt your brother?" Alice asked as gently as she could.

Doc shook his head, at a loss. "As far as I knew, he was a good man, an excellent doctor, a scientist. I have no idea what he'd gotten into or who he'd come across over the past four decades. All I can think is that he crossed the wrong person somehow."

Alice took a seat in the chair next to the bed. "And what about you? Do you know of anyone who might want to harm you?"

Alice was surprised when Doc answered very quickly. "Yes, I'm afraid I do."

Everyone leaned forward at this.

"Seriously?" asked Owen.

Doc nodded solemnly. "Woman named Idella Holcombe. She's furious with me."

"Why?" asked Franny.

"Because I lost her father last week." He looked up at them. "Willard Holcombe?"

"Willard Holcombe *died?*" said Owen. "Mr. Holcombe? From Lucky's Quik Pik?"

Lucky's was a handy little gas station-convenience store on the northeast edge of town, out toward Blue Lake. It was a great place to run for a slice of pizza, a half-gallon of milk, or a dozen eggs when you didn't want to go all the way over to Whitman's.

"Didn't say he died," said Doc. "I said I lost him." He let out a little groan. "Willard wanders off, you know. And I had him here at the hospital to run some tests last week—no big thing, but Willard doesn't like to be poked and prodded. Anyway, we lost him. We've been looking everywhere, but so far, no luck. And Idella, who's in town especially to encourage her dad, well . . . she came rushing into the hospital and really let me have it. Said I'd pay for being so careless."

"She could be our eyedrop-toting criminal!" said Owen. "What does she look like?"

"Oh . . . thin, about five foot five. Long white hair."

"Uh-oh," said Franny.

Mrs. Howard joined them in the room. "Dewey stopped off to take a phone call. He'll be in shortly," she said with a smile. She reached into her purse. "I have some mail here and I'll bet these holiday cards will cheer us."

"I'd be plenty cheerful if I could go home," said Doc.

Mrs. Howard gave him a look and proceeded to open the first card. "Oh look! Here's one from your Aunt Sophia in Palm Beach!"

The two read Aunt Sophia's latest news, then

flipped to the next card, which had come from an old friend in Williamsbridge, Vermont. Doc smiled over news of the little town up north, then tore open the next envelope. "Wonder who this one's from. There's no return address."

The front of the card was decorated with a cheerful wreath of holly. Doc opened it, read it, and looked up at his wife, his eyes wide.

"Dear? What is it? The color just left your face." Mrs. Howard reached over and read the card for herself. "Oh my." She dropped it onto the bed.

Owen quickly picked it up. He swallowed. "It's from . . . Doc's brother, Charles. It says, *I'm alive.*"

CHAPTER 8

The card had been postmarked three days earlier. As soon as Dewey arrived in the room, they handed it right over to him.

"So, he was trying to tell me," Doc said, a long, slow sigh escaping him. His shoulders sagged.

Alice's heart hurt for him. "I'm so sorry, Doc."

Doc gave her a wry smile. "In a way, it's comforting—knowing he wanted to reconnect after having to be away for so long. If only . . . well, we could've talked. About what our lives have been. About why in heaven's name he had to do what he did." He frowned. "About what he was doing in the barn." He shook his head sadly. "No use regretting it now, I guess. Won't bring him back."

"But at least you know he's with you in spirit,"

said Mrs. Howard, bending to plant a kiss on her husband's head.

Everyone said their goodbyes. Alice, Owen, and Franny were due on Main Street, where they'd be helping to set up for the big cookie exchange that was to take place that afternoon, and Dewey was headed back over to the station. Mrs. Howard promised to keep them posted about Doc's release, and they walked down the hall to the elevator.

Just as they arrived there, the door slid open with a *ding*. Inside the elevator was an attractive woman who looked to be in her early thirties, wearing a blazer and straight skirt, both in the same charcoal gray color as her shoes. Her hair was pulled into a tight bun at the nape of her neck and there was something uptight about her that Alice couldn't quite put her finger on. She looked up from her cellphone, catching sight of Dewey's uniform and badge first.

"Oh. Officer . . ." She leveled her gaze at the brass nametag beneath the badge. "Dewey. We spoke on the phone. I'm Ms. Portence."

"Of course!" said Dewey, quickly standing aside so that she could exit the elevator. "Let me show you to Dr. Howard's room. His wife is with him now. They know you're coming."

"Good," said Ms. Portence, with a curt nod.

She and Dewey walked back down the hall in the other direction, leaving Alice, Owen, and Franny standing at the open elevator.

"Aha! The mysterious visitor Dewey was telling Mrs. Howard about," said Owen. "Should we . . . wait for him to come back, do you think?"

"Definitely," said Franny as the empty elevator closed and went on its way without them. "I want to know who this Ms. Portence is."

A few moments later, Dewey returned to the elevator, a few fine drops of sweat visible at his temples.

"So?" Owen said, pressing the button to get the elevator back. "Who's the nice-if-somewhat-frightening lady?"

The door opened and they all got into the elevator.

"That's Ms. Portence," said Dewey as the door glided shut.

"So, we gathered," said Owen, cocking a brow at him.

"She's with the U. S. Marshals. She's here to talk to the Howards about Doc's brother."

Alice gasped. "She's with the—"

The elevator door opened, and Dewey cleared his throat loudly. They all walked silently through the crowded lobby and out the front door.

"That woman is with the U.S. Marshals?" Alice asked. "What does she want with the Howards? Was Doc's brother mixed up in something serious?"

"Other than being fake-dead for the past four decades," added Owen.

"Well, as it turns out," Dewey paused and cleared his throat, "it was all orchestrated. The wreck, the reports of the older Howard brother's death, the whole thing. Dr. Howard—Charles, that is—was put into the U. S. Federal Witness Protection Program and has been alive all this time, living in Portland, Oregon."

"That's incredible," said Alice. "And even Doc didn't know?"

"Apparently not," said Dewey. "But as next of kin, Doc is now being informed of exactly what happened and why. It'll all make sense to him and Mrs. H pretty soon."

"So, you know why Charles was in the witness protection program?" said Owen, giving Dewey a sideways glance. When Dewey hesitated, he prompted, "Gannon, tell us what you know."

"Well . . . you are knee deep in all of this, I guess. But it doesn't go any further than this conversation. Got it?"

Everyone nodded. They were just passing St.

Helena's at the corner of Phlox and Main, and instead of turning to go downtown on Main Street, they turned north and stepped into the quiet wooded cemetery behind the church.

"So," said Dewey, glancing around furtively, "apparently Charles Howard, who was still in his twenties back when he moved to New York City, saw something he shouldn't have."

"I grew up in New York. Believe me, I saw things I shouldn't have all the time," said Owen with a snort.

"See, Charles was still this small town boy in the big city back then," said Dewey. "According to Ms. Portence, he got lost and wandered right into the middle of a meeting between members of the mafia just as they were making plans for a drug smuggling operation. Charles didn't think they'd seen him, because it was dark, but he went straight to the police and reported what he'd witnessed. Led to a big bust and the incarceration of one of the high-ups in the organization—guy by the name of Willy B. Good."

"Willy B. Good?" said Owen, suppressing a laugh. "Please."

"And recently, old Willy died under mysterious circumstances at a maximum security prison," said Dewey.

"So that's why Charles thought it was safe to

come out of hiding," said Alice. "The person he was most afraid of was no longer a threat."

"Exactly," said Dewey, pointing at her. "All these years, he's been living and working in Portland, Oregon. Ms. Portence said he'd been married but didn't have any children, and his wife passed away a few years back. So, he was thinking, now that the coast was clear so to speak, he could come home and reconnect with his brother and the community he'd grown up in."

"Why be so sneaky about it? Rummaging around in Doc's barn. Sending him that Christmas card." Alice frowned. "Why not just walk up and knock on the door?"

"Because he'd been advised not to," said Dewey. "The U.S. Marshals weren't at all sure it would be entirely safe. There were other people who might pose a threat—even though the main one was gone. And coming out of the program, there's a process to go through. Charles was ready to take the risk, but he didn't want to endanger anyone else, so he came to Blue Valley, but then hesitated to come forward right away. Ms. Portence was supposed to meet up with him and go over how the transition process might best work, and he had let her know he'd be hiding out in the barn. Told her there was a spot he'd hidden in as a kid behind a panel in the wall and that if anyone spotted him, he'd duck in there. He didn't want to risk checking into any hotels or going into restaurants and things like that until he'd met with Ms. Portence. And I guess as anxious as he was to see his brother, he couldn't take the risk of putting him or Mrs. Howard into any kind of danger."

"So, he did what he could do," said Owen. "Like sending that card."

"Yep," said Dewey. "But there's more. Ms. Portence says she has colleagues watching the borders of town very closely, and that the killer is very likely still here, trying to blend in and act like just another tourist. She said it's probably someone connected with Willy B. Good—someone out for revenge who got wind that the man who sent old Willy up the river was still alive and moving across the country. I mean, there's no way Charles could've gotten from Portland to Blue Valley without being seen. Someone figured out he was here and killed him."

"I still think there's a good chance that the same person is responsible for both Doc's sickness and his brother's death," said Owen. "I mean, the two of them were practically twins. What if the person who tried to poison Doc realized they'd gotten the wrong man, so came back and got his brother—this time stabbing him instead of using the old eyedrop trick?"

Dewey nodded. "It's a definite possibility. Someone who didn't really know Charles but had seen his photo could've certainly gone after Doc by mistake."

"That is, if it wasn't Idella Holcombe who tried to get Doc," said Alice.

"Idella Holcombe?" asked Dewey. "Any relation to Willard? That man has us on a merry chase."

Franny slapped her forehead. "We got so wrapped up in the business with Ms. Portence that we forgot to tell you. Idella is Willard's daughter. She came to town to help her dad out while he underwent whatever tests Doc was planning to run on him—and she's furious with Doc for losing him. She even told him he'd pay for what he'd done."

"And she has long white hair," added Alice. "Just like the figure we all saw running away from the barn last night."

"Oh my gosh!" Owen clapped a hand over his mouth. "What if the killer *wasn't* someone who was mistaking Doc for Charles, but was instead someone who was mistaking Charles for Doc? Old Idella tried poisoning Doc with those cookies, but then saw someone she *thought* was Doc snooping around the barn at the Howards' house. The poison obviously hadn't worked, so—"

"So, she stabbed him," said Dewey nodding. He quickly radioed Officer Trimble, instructing him to call every hotel and inn and find out where Idella Holcombe was staying. He put his radio back into its holster. "We'll locate this woman and talk to her. Meanwhile, be careful. Any tourist you see could still be the killer. So, I don't care whether they're a customer in your shop, a passerby on the street, or an entrant in your Christmas cookie exchange—*you be careful*."

CHAPTER 9

It was hard to believe the Holiday Cookie Exchange had started out as a simple plan to get a few friends together and swap cookies. Owen and Alice's mother, Bea, stood at the registration table, both looking pleased as punch.

"Would you look at that crowd?" Owen said, watching the cookie bakers milling about.

"You might be gloating just a little bit," said Alice, nudging Owen.

"Hey, Bea and I are the dream team when it comes to cookies, as you can see," said Owen, sweeping an arm across the expanse of long tables they'd set up on Main Street, which closed to cars for the festival. "People are here from all over— and not just all over Tennessee, either."

"Everyone loves a cookie exchange," Bea sang. She smiled at Alice. "I can't wait to one day bake cookies with my grandchildren."

"I even bought Theo his own mini kitchen for Christmas," said Owen.

"He's going to love that," said Franny, who was doing a booming business at the Joe's hot cocoa and wassail booth, which she and Beth had set up right next to the cookie registration table. Beth had gone back over to Joe's while Franny ran the booth. Theo had joined in the fun as well. Franny had set him up in his highchair behind her counter. The two were wearing matching red-and-white striped scarves, and Theo was keeping busy charming the customers. Franny handed a pair of ladies their steaming cups of cocoa, and Theo clapped and said *bye-bye* when they left with their purchases, which pleased the ladies to no end.

Festive music played over the speakers they'd set up, and every table was covered with platter after platter of festive cookies and highlighted by the lovely centerpieces Mrs. Howard had teamed up with Violet Garcia, owner of Violet's Blooms and Bouquets, to create.

"Too bad Mrs. Howard isn't here to see this," Owen lamented. "But I'm texting her lots of photos."

"And I've already gathered a whole slew of recipes to take to her," said Bea.

Each cookie platter had a stack of recipe cards next to it. Every registrant had been given a basket, so that they could walk from table to table, sampling cookies and gathering recipes. At the moment, people seemed to be having the most fun just mixing and mingling with other cookie enthusiasts, sharing their secret ingredients, and decorating ideas.

Officer Dewey hurried up to the registration table, a platter of cookies covered in plastic wrap in his hands. "Am I too late? I got tied up at the station."

"Of course, you're not too late!" said Bea, taking out her clipboard and scanning the list of names. "You're all preregistered, Dewey. You may place your cookies on table three, in slot F."

"Got it," said Dewey.

"Here's your basket for collecting recipes and samples, and here's your official cookie baker badge." She looked at her daughter. "Alice, dear, give Dewey a hand."

Alice nodded and took the tray off Dewey's hands, then led him over to table three.

"Dewey these look delicious!" she said, as she pulled off the plastic wrap and admired the tiny, round shortbread cookies, each one studded with a cherry in the middle.

"Try one," said Dewey. "I brought extra."

Alice popped one of the buttery cookies into her mouth and chewed. "Oh boy," she said, looking at Dewey. "I think these are going to replace pie as my biggest pregnancy craving."

"I call them Little Cherry Bells," said Dewey. "I'm so glad you like them. I know this isn't a contest or anything, but I still want to, you know, hold my own against the other cookies."

"I had no idea you were a baker." Alice took one more cookie, promising herself it would be her last.

"Since I was a kid," said Dewey, nodding.

"Let's walk around and look at some of the other entrants," said Alice. "Grab your basket."

As they walked around, admiring and tasting, Franny caught up with them.

"I have a little break," she said. "We ran out of everything if you can believe that. Beth's coming over with fresh batches of cocoa and wassail. Thought I'd try a cookie or two while I'm waiting." She grinned and swiped a chocolate-dipped macaroon from a tray.

"Where's Theo?" asked Alice.

"Mom and Dad came and got him," said Franny.

"Hey, wait for me!" Owen hurried over.

"Thought you were too busy lording over the cookies," joked Alice.

"Hey, my work is pretty much done," said Owen, holding up his hands. "Every registrant is checked in, and now it's just a matter of tasting and having a good time."

They walked on, stopping now and then to admire a particularly delicious looking cookie or to talk to the various bakers. They knew many of them, as the whole town had basically showed up for the exchange. But well over half of the participants were out-of-towners, and Alice knew that meant the inns and hotels were booked, the shops were doing a brisk business, and the restaurants were hopping. A successful Hometown Holidays Festival was a boon to the whole town.

Up ahead, they noticed Pearl Ann and Marge raving about one particular cookie they'd both just tried. Ethel Primrose, director of the Blue Valley Heritage Museum, was just saying she wanted to see what all the fuss was about and pushed her way up to the platter to pick up a cookie. When she did, Alice, Owen, and Franny—as well as Officer Dewey—froze momentarily.

"Stop, Ethel!" Alice said, rushing forward.

Ethel had been about to put a very distinct cookie

into her mouth—one that was shaped like a candy cane, made of red and white cookie doughs that had been intertwined to resemble stripes. It looked *exactly* like the cookies that had made Doc sick.

"What are you talking about, Alice?" said Pearl Ann. "These cookies are amazing!" She reached over and took one of the recipe cards next to the platter. "We keep coming back to them. I think I've eaten about a dozen!"

"How do you feel?" asked Dewey.

"Great!" said Pearl Ann, giving him a puzzled look.

Dewey breathed a sigh of relief.

Alice took one of the recipe cards. "These were submitted by someone from New York!" Her hear pounded in her chest, thinking about how Charles Howard had lived in New York when he'd witnessed the crime that had driven him into the witness protection program. She flipped the card over. "The person who baked them is Donna Rizzo."

Dewey snatched the card out of her hand and read it for himself. He gulped.

"What is it Dewey?" asked Pearl Ann. "You know this woman? Because I'd like to meet her and tell her how much we love her cookies."

Dewey cleared his throat. "I'll let you know if I

see her." He hurried away. Alice, Owen, and Franny followed after him.

Once they were clear of the crowd, Alice tugged at Dewey's shirt sleeve. "Dewey slow down! Where are you going?"

Dewey pulled out his cell phone. "I'm calling Ms. Portence."

"So, you know who this Donna Rizzo is?" asked Owen.

Dewey paused in his dialing and looked at them. "Remember how I told you Charles Howard had testified against a man known as Willy B. Good?"

"How could we forget?" said Owen.

"Well, the man's real name was William Bertrand Rizzo."

"Shouldn't we get those cookies off the table?" asked Franny.

"Those cookies are a huge hit," said Dewey. "Everyone's been eating them all afternoon, and no one is sick. I'd say it's safe to conclude that only Doc's batch was poisoned—that is, if they were, indeed, baked by the same person. Right now, all I want to do is find this Donna Rizzo."

"Well that part is easy," said Owen. "I met her earlier when she registered. She won't be hard to spot

. . ." He scanned the crowd. "Yep. She's right over there."

They all walked over to where the woman, who was dressed in green and red from head to toe, was walking along, her basket full of recipes and cookies. She was wearing a very snug green miniskirt that looked to be made out of some sort of synthetic suede, paired with a bright red sweater which was studded all over with tiny jingle bells. Over the sweater she'd added a wide black belt with a metal buckle that looked like something Santa himself would wear and had finished the ensemble off with a Santa hat and boots. Her wrists were covered with bracelets that jingled as she reached for a cookie.

"Hello, Ms. Rizzo," Owen said with a friendly smile.

She turned and looked at him. "Hello. Oh—I met you earlier, didn't I?"

"Yes," said Owen. "When you registered. Your cookies are a huge hit!"

She gave him a huge smile. "Are they?"

"Everyone's talking about them," said Franny.

"Oh my, well that's just fabulous!" She put a hand to her heart. "Mother would be proud. It's her recipe, you know. She always made them at the holidays."

Dewey stepped forward, and Donna frowned at the sight of his uniform. "Oh. Hello."

"Hello, Ms. Rizzo. I'm afraid I'm going to have to ask you to come with me down to the station. It's only a short walk that way." He pointed toward Phlox Street.

"Now just hold your horses! Are you *arresting* me? What for?"

"No, no!" Dewey waved his hands around, his face turning red all the way to the tips of his ears. "I'm not arresting you. I need to ask you some questions is all. I think it'd be easier to do that away from this crowd of people."

Donna stamped her booted foot. "No, it wouldn't. You got something to ask me, you can ask me here."

"Okay . . . Are you any relation to William Rizzo, a.k.a. Willy B. Good, from New York?"

"I am," Donna said without hesitation. "He's my brother. That's why I'm in this town. I'm looking for . . . well, *was* looking for someone who had a connection to Willy. But now I'll never find him."

"What happened?" asked Owen.

"He died," said Donna, who was clearly not the type to beat around the bush.

"You're talking about Dr. Charles Howard," said Dewey.

"How did you know that?" Donna stamped the boot again. "Oh yeah right. Let me guess. Small town. You're probably all in each other's business. That's how it is in my neighborhood back home."

"Well," said Dewey, who was beginning to get irritated, "I am a police officer, and there was a murder in my town. Of course, I know about it."

"Look, I had nothing to do with Charles Howard's death. I came to this town because I heard through the grapevine that he was alive and had been seen here." She leaned toward Owen and said in a lower voice, "I also heard about this cookie exchange and figured what the heck? I'm a passionate cookie baker and I'm going to get all kinds of new recipes to take home. Might as well do something fun while I'm in town, you know?"

"I get it," said Owen. "I'm a passionate cookie baker, too. Come by my bakery, Sourdough, while you're in town."

"Will do!" said Donna, looking extremely pleased at the prospect. "I walked by there this morning. I could smell the fresh bread all the way out on the sidewalk!"

"Baked fresh every day," said Owen. "By the way, I grew up in the city."

"You did? Which part?"

Dewey cleared his throat. "If we could get back to the questioning, please?"

"Oh. Sorry." Donna turned her attention back to Dewey. "So, as I was saying, I came to town to see Charles Howard."

"To kill him?" said Dewey.

"No! To thank him."

Her answer took everyone by surprise.

"Thank him for what?" asked Dewey.

Donna looked around, then led them all over to a quiet spot further from the cookie tables. "You probably already know that Charles had testified against Willy way back in the day. Well, going to jail was the best thing that ever happened to my brother. His whole life turned around and he repented! He made amends with the family, with old friends. He was a better man for the whole experience."

"Sorry to hear he died," said Alice, reaching out to pat Donna on the arm.

Donna shook her head. "Oh, he didn't die," she said. "Once he was finally on the straight and narrow, he really got a conscience. And recently, he . . . well, he let the authorities know the names of a few key players . . . he did the right thing, okay? And then he left the country. He entered a monastery in Tibet. He's living a whole new life now. That's all just between us, though, got it?"

Everyone nodded.

Dewey raised his hand. "So, the reports that he'd died in prison . . ."

"Were greatly exaggerated, yes," said Donna.

Dewey frowned. "But there's still a question about your cookies," he said. "Thing is, a member of our community—who happens to be the brother of Charles Howard—received a tin of cookies that looked exactly like yours. And they were doused with tetrahydrozoline, and they made him very sick."

"Somebody *eyedropped* the guy? How awful!" Donna's eyes grew wide.

"And the thing is," Alice said, "our Doc Howard looks very much like his brother Charles. So, we're thinking maybe the cookies went to the wrong Howard brother?"

"Wait a second. So *that's* what happened to the other batch of cookies." Donna clenched her jaw and shook her small fist, jingling the many bracelets on her wrist. "I'll kill her!"

"What are you saying?" said Dewey.

"That I bet I know who sent the cookies to your friend. And I'd be glad to take you to her right now."

CHAPTER 10

Following Donna Rizzo's car as it tore down Trout Lily and hung a sharp right onto Phlox was not an easy thing to do.

"Oh my gosh! Did you see that? Smoke just came up from her tires!" Owen, who was seated in the front seat of Dewey's squad car swiveled to face Dewey in the driver's seat. "Hey, how about we turn on the siren?"

Dewey swatted Owen's hand away from the switch. "I already told you we're not turning on the siren. *Or* the lights. Although if she goes any faster, I'm going to have to give her a speeding ticket."

The radio sputtered to life. "Dewey? Trimble here. You read? Over."

Dewey reached out and tapped a button. "Yep. What've you got?"

"I finally found out where Idella Holcombe's staying. She'd—" The line turned to static.

Dewey grumbled something under his breath and tapped at the radio. "Trimble? You there?"

Just then, Donna veered off of Phlox onto Lake Trail, the little road that circled Blue Lake.

"Oh look—I can see our houses across the water," said Owen, pointing to the east end of the lake as they cleared Town Dock. The lake houses where the three friends lived when they weren't in their Main Street apartments lay to their right, but Donna had taken the left fork off Lake Trail, whizzing past the houses on the west bank.

"This is what a bat out of hell must feel like," said Franny from the backseat.

Within a few seconds, they were pulling into the parking lot at Cozy Bear Camp and Glamp, an upscale campground complete with hiking trails, and a favorite destination with the tourists.

They leapt out of the car and jogged to catch up to Donna, who was stalking through the arched entrance, which was now swagged with seasonal garlands and twinkling lights. They passed the small cabin where guests checked in or stopped off for firewood, sundries, or Cozy Bear t-shirts. Harv and Sue Anderson, who owned the place, popped out of the cabin.

"What's up?" Harv asked, trying to keep up with the growing parade.

"We're not sure," said Dewey.

By that time, Donna was on the wooden deck outside one of the fanciest glamping tents at Cozy Bear. She threw open the door. "Lafonda Rizzo! You have some explaining to do!" She stomped through the door.

They heard another voice from inside the glamping tent. "Geez, Donna, I'm trying to take a nap here! Aren't you supposed to be at that cookie thing all afternoon?"

"Outside! Now!" said Donna, and she emerged from the tent dragging another woman behind her. "Everyone, this is Lafonda Rizzo. Lafonda, this is everyone. Now. Why don't you tell these nice people why you stole and then poisoned a batch of my candy cane cookies?" She squeezed Lafonda's arm, lowered her voice, and ground out, "And I swear, Lafonda, if you had anything to do with killing that Charles Howard guy you are going straight to prison! He was a good man just trying to do the right thing!"

Just like Donna, Lafonda was dressed in very striking clothes—a black pencil skirt with black stockings and a purple sweater. Her hair—also like Donna's—had definitely been dyed black, and she looked younger from farther away than she did up close.

"Doing the right thing? Sending my Willy up the river? Donna! Shame on you—you are Willy's sister!"

"Lafonda! My brother was a criminal, may I remind you, and he wasn't *your* Willy. You were divorced, remember? And that was like forty years ago!" She shook her head angrily. "You're just mad because you didn't get his money."

"Well . . . now that he's gone, it seems like I, as his only wife, should be entitled to—"

"Listen, sister, I've got news for you," said Donna. "Willy didn't have any money and he's not even dead!"

Lafonda's face went entirely blank.

"That's right! Not. Even. Dead."

"What are you saying to me, Donna?"

"Willy's in a monastery. In Tibet. He's found a whole new life."

"A new life, huh?" Lafonda's face was turning purple with rage. "I'll give him a new life! And then I'll kill him!" She looked at Dewey. "You hear that officer? I'm going to commit murder, I am going to kill Willy G., and I don't care if I go to jail for it! That scumbag!"

"Ms., uh, Rizzo," Dewey started to say.

"I don't want to hear that name ever again! I'm taking back my maiden name, after all these years." She looked skyward and shook her fist. "From here on out, I'm Lafonda Loretti Bianchi De Luca!"

"Okay, Ms., uh . . ." Dewey didn't even attempt to call her by name.

"That's fine, call me Lafonda," she said, popping a stick of gum into her mouth and checking her nails, which were very long and painted in bright purple to match her sweater.

"Why did you beg to come on this trip with me, Lafonda?" said Donna, shoving Dewey to the side. "Just so you could kill that nice man?"

"Kill him? Have you gone out of your mind, Donna? I didn't kill anyone!" She examined her nails more closely and mumbled, "I just . . . wanted to see the man who put my Willy away." She looked at Alice. "And this was before I found out he was a scumbag who went to Tibet without even telling his *wife*, you understand."

Alice nodded rapidly.

"Ex-wife," Donna corrected. "Get over it, Lafonda!"

"Oh, I promise you I *am* over it, Donna!"

"Fine!"

"Fine!"

The two women looked at one another silently for a moment, and then Lafonda, tucking a frizzy strand of hair behind her ear, seemed to soften a bit. "You're still my sister, though, right?" she said hopefully.

Donna sighed. "Yes, I'm still your sister." She opened her arms and the two embraced.

"Wait. What just happened here?" said Owen.

"But Lafonda, did you or did you not kill Charles Howard?"

"I'm telling you, I didn't kill anyone," Lafonda said in a tiny voice. "I just wanted to see him, to teach him a little lesson. I was going to tell him off, but I lost my nerve. I was going to give him a piece of my mind. For Willy's sake, you know?" She looked over at Alice again. "And this was before I knew he was—"

"A scumbag," Alice said, nodding.

There was a moment of silence before Donna said, "Lafonda, don't you listen to the local news? It was on the radio this morning. Charles Howard is dead. He was stabbed!"

Lafonda, clearly taken aback, gasped. "I didn't

stab anybody!" She looked at Dewey. "You have to believe me!"

"Did you steal a batch of my cookies, put eyedrops on them, and try to poison anybody?"

"What? Are you out of your mind? I would never —well, there was that time back in my twenties when I—but no! I swear I didn't take your cookies!"

"Then who did?" said Donna.

Lafonda, who was beginning to panic, turned to Dewey. "Oh, please don't send me to jail! I didn't steal cookies or stab anybody or poison anybody! I'm innocent!"

Donna stepped protectively in front of her ex-sister-in-law, facing Dewey. "We want to help you," she said. "Let us help you find the person who killed Charles Howard. Then we'll go back home, and you can all go on with your lives. Please."

"Someone must have had a serious beef with the man," said Lafonda, putting her hands on her hips. "They were even madder at him than I was, to stab him like that." She shook her head.

Just then, a branch snapped nearby. Alice looked toward the wooded trails that started at the edge of the campground. She sucked in a breath. There, hiding behind a large tree, watching them, was a small, thin woman with long white hair.

CHAPTER 11

The chase was on—and when Alice thought about the whole scene later, she couldn't help but laugh. The little silver-haired lady went running down Hemlock Trail, a veritable parade of people in her wake and gaining on her fast. Dewey and Owen led the way. Harv and Sue were close behind them, trying to advise them about upcoming shortcuts or pitfalls in the trail. These were followed by the Rizzo sisters, who were jingling and yelling the whole time, their city accents more out of place than ever in the quiet Tennessee woods. Alice and Franny brought up the rear, Franny reminding Alice that she was six months pregnant and needed to slow down. For her part, Alice was more waddling than running, and was out of breath by the time they'd even reached the trailhead.

It wasn't long before Idella Holcombe realized she was outmatched and gave up. She stood, hands on her knees, silver hair falling forward into her face, panting.

"Idella Holcombe, I presume," said Dewey, triumphantly taking her by the arm.

Just then, Dewey's radio sputtered from his shoulder holster. "Dewey? It's Trimble. Can you hear me now? Over."

Dewey rolled his eyes and took the radio into his hand. "What is it, Trimble?"

"I was trying to tell you before. I located that Idella Holcombe. She's staying out at Cozy Bear. Want me to head over there and look for her?"

Dewey sighed. "I'm already here. I have the suspect in hand."

"What?" Trimble cleared his throat. "I mean, that's great. Need backup? Over."

Dewey looked at the assembled group. "I've got backup out the wazoo. We'll be there shortly. You be ready for us."

"Got it. Over and out."

Dewey took out his handcuffs. "Idella Holcombe,

I'm taking you to the police station for questioning related to the murder of Charles Howard."

Idella took one look at the handcuffs and began to sob. "You have to believe me, Officer! I had no idea he'd die! I promise you this wasn't murder! I didn't mean to kill him!"

"Well, that's generally what happens when you stab someone right through the heart," said Owen.

"Stab someone—wait! What are you talking about?" She pointed a boney finger at Owen.

Owen shifted uncomfortably. "That's how he was murdered. With a big old knife."

"But—but—" Idella's bottom lip quivered. "I was only trying to make him sick because he lost my dad! I didn't *stab* anyone!"

Dewey let out an exasperated sigh. "Are you talking about Doc and the eyedrop-laced cookies?"

Idella nodded. "I didn't even bake the cookies. That lady over there was unloading her things and she left some cookies outside her tent." She pointed at Donna, who put her hands on her hips in outrage. "I wanted to teach Dr. Howard a lesson, so I, well—I"— she looked apologetically at Donna. "I swiped one tin of the cookies." She looked back at Dewey and pleaded, "But she had so many of them, I didn't think they'd be missed! I sprinkled eyedrops into them—I saw this show on TV where someone did that to make someone sick—and I put a gift tag on them and left them for Dr. Howard to find at his office. Then later, I realized I shouldn't have done it. It was stupid of me. I mean, Dad wanders off. It's not really the doctor's fault." She kicked at a rock. "Well, it sort of is. But anyway, I was walking along over by the hospital, searching for Dad one more time . . . this was Friday night. It was dark, but I heard a noise, like voices or something. I looked over and saw the doctor moving around in that barn. I figured that must be his house next to it—his last name is on the mailbox. Plus, I already knew his practice was right next door. So I went over to the barn, just to tell him not to eat those cookies." She held up her hands in innocence. "I went inside . . . it was all shadowy, and I tripped over something." She grimaced. "I landed on the floor right next to this dark shape, but I couldn't tell what it was, so I turned on the flashlight on my phone." She put a hand to her chest. "And there he was, lying on the ground. I almost screamed! I thought maybe . . . well, maybe I'd accidentally killed him. So, I ran away."

This revelation was met with wide eyes all around.

Finally, Dewey put his handcuffs away. "Okay.

First, Idella, Doc Howard—the man you gave the cookies to—is not dead. He's going to be fine, but you did make him sick, and it'll be up to him whether or not charges are pressed."

"Not dead? Oh, thank heaven!" Idella wailed.

"Second," Dewey continued, "The man you saw in Doc's barn was actually his brother, Charles. He was murdered."

"By way of a knife through the heart," Owen intoned, getting him a sharp look from Dewey.

"Now Idella, this is important. I want you to think back. Did you see anyone else when you were in the barn?"

Idella slowly shook her head. "I didn't see anybody, but I did find something strange. The, uh, thing I tripped over. I'd touched it after I fell, before I realized I was lying there next to a dead man." She looked at Dewey. "I only took it with me because my fingerprints were on it, and I was afraid I'd be a suspect." She sniffed and mumbled, "Of course, at the time I thought I'd killed the guy, so there's that."

"Idella, what was it?"

"A book—an old high school annual."

"And where is it now?"

"I hid it. In my tent."

"Can you go get it, please?"

Alice could tell by the tiny quaver in Dewey's voice that he was trying to be patient.

Idella nodded and jogged off to her campsite—far more modest than the Rizzos' beautiful glamping tent. She returned and handed the book over to Dewey. Everyone squeezed in closer to have a look.

"An old Blue Valley High School annual!" said Franny. "Wow—that's from like forty-eight years ago!"

"Look up Charles Howard!" said Alice.

Dewey flipped through the book. "Howard, Howard, How—Here it is. Oh. No, that's not Charles. That's David Howard, sophomore."

"Doc!" said Alice. "He was a couple years behind his brother. Flip to the senior class."

When Dewey started to flip in that direction, the book opened to the correct page. But they couldn't see Charles Howard's photo. There was a big black X drawn over his face—or at least over the half that was still intact. The page had been ripped right down the center of his photo.

"All this time, I've been thinking this murder had something to do with whatever it was that landed Charles in the witness protection program," said Dewey. "But now . . ." He snapped the high school

Doc Howard was home from the hospital. Mrs. Howard texted the group as they were driving back into town from Cozy Bear. As it was almost dinnertime, it was decided that they'd make a quick stop at the Smiling Hound and pick up Doc's favorite—the Captain of the Sea platter. Alice, Owen, and Dewey waited for the to-go box while Franny made a quick run to her parents' house to pick up Theo. Then they all made the short walk to the Howards'.

"Like the man needs any more food in the house," said Owen with a roll of his eyes. "Half the town will have dropped off casseroles and cakes by now."

"But this is his favorite," said Alice, holding up the Smiling Hound box.

"I feel perfectly fine," Doc insisted after they'd all

come inside and joined him in the living room, where Mrs. Howard had him all set up in his favorite armchair with a stack of books and magazines, extra pillows, the television remote control, and several bouquets of flowers with *Get Well Soon* balloons attached to them. "I don't need to lay around too much. Not good for the body."

"You're *resting*," said Mrs. Howard, giving him a stern look. "That's not the same thing as laying around."

"Isn't it?"

"Listen to me, Dr. Howard," she said, using her high school English teacher voice. "You need to take a big dose of your own medicine. You always tell your patients to rest."

"She's right about that. You do," said Alice.

"I'll tell you what. If you take it easy today and tomorrow morning and afternoon, you can go down to the community center for play rehearsals tomorrow evening. Fair?" said Mrs. Howard.

"That's fair, I guess," said Doc.

"Besides, tonight you can help us without even getting up," said Dewey, coming forward with the yearbook. "This was found in the barn right after your brother's death. Have you seen it before, by any chance?"

Doc took the book into his hands. "Well of course I have. This is one of the annuals from when I was in high school." He turned it over, then glanced toward the bookshelves that lined the wall to his left. "We have a copy of this same book, right over there."

"Haven't looked at this volume in years," said Mrs. Howard.

"Who does this one belong to?" Doc flipped to the opening pages.

"Those pages have been ripped out," said Dewey. "We've looked through it a few times and can't find anything that would make it clear who owns it. I dusted it for prints, of course, but at this point, we still don't know whose it is. The prints we found aren't on record."

"Whoever it was was certainly no fan of my brother's," said Doc, looking at the page with Charles's photo—or what was left of it.

"Do you remember from back in high school if there was anyone who might still hold a monster grudge against your brother?" asked Owen.

Doc paused and looked at him. "I hate to point fingers. But there absolutely was one person in particular." He shook his head. "I hate to say . . ."

"Doc, trust me," said Dewey, "if they're innocent, nothing will come of you telling this."

Doc sighed and looked up at Mrs. Howard. "There's Samantha."

She nodded. "Dr. McCorkle."

"I had a feeling she wasn't too nuts about him," said Alice, remembering the doctor's reaction when Charles's name had been mentioned. "What's that all about?"

"Those two had gone to school together from kindergarten all the way through med school," said Doc. "They were close friends, but they were also competitors from the very beginning—in everything. Why, I even remember them competing in the pie-eating competition at one of our Annual Independence Day weekends." He chuckled. "Charles just managed to edge Samantha out, but she had him on the ropes for a while there. But most of all, they competed academically. Anyway, there was a final straw . . . and I don't think Samantha ever spoke to Charles again after that."

He glanced at his wife again, and she gave him a nod of assurance.

"Don't want to throw a colleague under the bus or anything," he muttered before turning back to Dewey. "That job my brother took in New York? It was a post at a very prestigious research hospital. Samantha had applied for it first and in her excitement, had told Charles about it. Then he applied . . ."

"And sealed the deal," guessed Owen.

"Exactly. She felt he'd betrayed her in the worst way."

"Judging by the way she looked like she'd just bitten into a lemon at the mention of his name, I'd say she never got over it," said Franny, giving Theo a little kiss on the top of his fuzzy head. He'd long since fallen asleep in his stroller.

"We'll confront Dr. McCorkle," said Dewey. "Is there anyone else you can think of? Anyone at all who had a tumultuous relationship with your brother?"

"Other than Samantha, no. Except for Annabelle Swift. He was engaged to her, but she ended it just before he moved to New York."

"Ms. Swift. Teacher at the high school," Dewey confirmed. "I had her for calculus." He looked pained. "Lowest grade I got the whole four years."

"That's Annabelle," said Mrs. Howard, placing a napkin, fork, and knife on a TV tray and setting it up in front of Doc. She then put his Sea Captain's Platter in front of him and opened the lid.

"Oh, this is fantastic. My favorite!" said Doc, tucking his napkin in under his chin.

"I gathered that the relationship had problems, since the two were engaged and then broke up," said Dewey.

"Did Ms. Swift ever marry?" asked Owen.

"She did," said Mrs. Howard. "And divorced. Twice. Took back her maiden name, Swift, after the second husband."

"So, love has been a rocky road for her since way back," said Franny.

"Yes," said Mrs. Howard. "I think she's resigned herself to staying single for now." She put a hand on her husband's shoulder. "Everyone can't be as lucky as Doc and me, I suppose."

They stayed and visited a while longer, Doc devouring his Sea Captain's platter, looking fit as a fiddle. Then they headed outside into the chilly evening air. Franny tucked a warm blanket around Theo, who was just waking up, ready for his evening snack.

"Luke and Ben will be home tomorrow," said Franny. "I'm sure you'll all get this thing solved soon."

"I'd like to get it solved *before* they get home," said Dewey. "Cases like this can get cold really fast. And I feel like we're getting close."

They arrived at the corner of Phlox and Main,

where Dewey said goodnight and continued on to the station, and everyone else turned down Main to go home.

"We have two solid suspects to consider," said Franny.

"We need to confront both Annabelle Swift and Samantha McCorkle," said Alice.

"Rattle their cages and see what happens," agreed Owen. "I have an idea."

CHAPTER 13

Sunday morning was the perfect time for Owen's plan to come into play. The night before, after returning to their apartments and tucking Theo into bed, Alice, Owen, and Franny had met outside in the rooftop garden, where they'd opened Alice's red binder to check the schedule of events and lists of volunteers for the next day.

"That's what I thought," said Alice, tapping her finger on the laminated page. "Both Annabelle and Samantha are signed up to help with the library's holiday fundraiser—the Merry Book-mas Market." She ran her finger down the page. "Oh—and they're also both helping out with the play rehearsal at the community center tomorrow evening. Annabelle's on costumes and Samantha's on props."

"Convenient that they signed up for the same events," said Owen, tenting his fingers.

"But not surprising," said Alice. "They went to high school together, after all. They're longtime friends. I've seen them having lunch at the Parkview Café plenty of times."

"Ooh. Maybe they plotted Charles Howard's murder together," said Owen.

They called the Rizzo women and asked if they were still willing to help, and both gladly agreed.

"I, for one, want to sock it to whoever killed Charlie," said Donna.

"If she's in, I'm in," added Lafonda.

Alice could hear their bracelets jingling in the background.

The next morning, they all met at the Paper Owl, where they went over the plan. The Rizzos would be the official cage-rattlers since neither Samantha nor Annabelle knew them. Donna had shown up wearing another tiny skirt—this one red with a fluffy white trim around the hem, and a green sweater with the words *Santa's Favorite* spelled out in sequins across the front. Lafonda, on the other hand, was wearing a green skirt with glittering holly berries sewn all over it, paired with a red sweater, her sequins spelling the words *Nice and Naughty*. Of course, they'd accessorized appropriately. There were charm bracelets, jingle bell necklaces, and festive hair ornaments.

"We'll all meet back here in, say, an hour?" said Owen.

"Perfect," said Franny, bouncing Theo in his carrier. "Theo and I are off to make a big batch of wake-up mocha cocoa for our morning customers, aren't we, my little elf?"

When Theo laughed, Franny did as well, and Alice heard her telling him how Daddy would be home that evening as she walked back into Joe's, which made Alice's heart sing. Thankfully, the weather in the Nashville area was clearing up, and soon, Luke would be home too, and they could all relax and enjoy the countdown to Christmas together.

"And I have a ton of baking to do," said Owen.

"I'll be out at the park on patrol," Dewey said, looking from one Rizzo to the other. "Since the library fundraiser is there, I'll be nearby if you should need me."

The Rizzos gave each other a nod, squared their shoulders, and slipped out onto Main Street. Alice saw them checking their reflections in her front window, adding additional coats of lipstick before heading off toward the park. Dewey stepped out a minute later and went in the same direction.

The hour didn't fly by as it should have. Alice had plenty to do in the shop, helping customers and restocking shelves. Lacie and Zack arrived and went straight to work. Through the cased opening, the sounds of chatter and coffee cups clinking on saucers at Joe's stayed steady, with Franny's holiday music track looping in the background. Soon, Alice inhaled the telltale smells of a fresh batch of Owen's patented sin-amon rolls coming out of the oven. Her stomach growled.

"Don't worry, little one," she said, patting her belly. "Uncle Owen will have plenty of special treats for you once you're born."

Marge Hartfield stopped by with a fresh load of candles, including a case of Flicker Wix, her new battery-operated candles. These Alice tucked into her candle corner, along with a selection of Christmas story books and a smattering of official Joe's Coffee mugs. She smiled, thinking of how the Main Street shopkeepers supported one another. Marge, for instance, offered books about candles and yoga from the Paper Owl at the Waxy Wick. They were always sending customers each other's way.

After what seemed like an eternity, Donna Rizzo pushed open the front door, and came jingling into the bookshop. Alice told Lacie and Zack she was taking a break, texted Owen and Franny, and they all settled in at a corner table in the coffee shop.

"That Dr. McCorkle is guilty for sure," Donna said in a loud whisper. "At first, I thought she was going to be a tough nut to crack. But then, she completely spilled her guts."

"Back up," said Owen. "Start from the beginning, before the gut-spilling."

Donna nodded and took a sip of her coffee. "So, I spotted her based on your description of her and of course, she was wearing a nametag. Anyhow, I acted like I was browsing the merchandise." She held up a little shopping bag. "Do you think I could get reimbursed for this stuff?"

"No," said Owen.

"Can't blame a girl for trying," said Donna with a shrug. "So, I got her to warm up by asking her gift-giving advice for some of the people on my Christmas list. Then, I told her I'd have to be careful how much I spent, because I'd just lost a promotion at work to this jerk who wasn't even as qualified as me." She snorted. "That got her talking, all right."

"What'd she say?" asked Franny.

"Well at first, she sympathized. And when I rattled on for a while—about the injustice of it all and everything, she started getting angry—you know, like angry on my behalf on account of my being robbed of the promotion. But then when I asked if she'd ever been passed over, she turned redder than my skirt. Said she had, but that the jerk who stole her golden opportunity got what was coming to him." Donna leaned back in her seat and crossed her arms. "How about them apples?"

"She practically confessed!" said Owen. "Did you tell Dewey?"

"He heard the whole thing!" said Donna. "He was *patrolling*"—she put air quotes around the word— "about five feet away."

Just then, Lafonda came wandering through the cased opening. When she spotted the group in the corner, she sauntered over and took a seat.

"You'll never guess," she said in a low voice. "That Annabelle Swift? Guilty as sin!"

"What?" Donna swiveled in her seat to face Lafonda. "*My* suspect is guilty!"

"Not as guilty as mine," Lafonda insisted. "So. I asked Annabelle to help me pick out a gift for my no-good-dirty ex-husband. I was like, *what do you buy for the person you want to kill*?"

Donna snorted again. "Good one, Lafonda."

"Well of course that led to us talking about love and men and how they break our hearts. I'm telling you, maybe she was the one who broke up with old Charlie, but it's clear she still feels the effects of it. He must've done something awful to get her mad enough that she still flies into a rage forty-some-odd years later."

"She flew into a rage?" Alice asked.

"Her face turned so red I thought she would, like, spontaneously combust or something!"

"Mine did that too!" said Donna, slapping hands with Lafonda.

"Did you tell Dewey about this?" asked Franny.

"He heard it all," Lafonda confirmed. "I gave him a wink when I left the park. I felt like a real spy and all."

Theo could be heard waking up through the baby monitor Franny had set on the table.

"Oops. Better run upstairs and get my little guy," she said. "Drinks and cookies on the house," she told the Rizzos. "Even if we still don't have a clue who killed Charles Howard."

"No prob," said Owen, propping his elbows on the table. "We just have to launch plan B." He looked at Alice. "The show must go on!"

CHAPTER 14

"So, what's your Plan B, again?" asked Franny as they walked toward the theater early that evening.

"Plan A was to get our prime suspects stirred up about Charles, just to see how they'd react. Plan B is to shock them into confessing," said Owen. He led them over to the side door of the community center, which housed a very fine stage that was used for local theatrical productions, awards ceremonies, and the like. "After their run-ins with the Rizzos, I'd say both are primed and ready to blow."

Owen knocked in a particular rhythm, and the door creaked open.

"Come right in!" Doc's voice came from behind the door, which he held so that they could all enter. They'd come into the back of the center's kitchen—a space they'd all spent plenty of time in, baking and prepping food for various community events. But as the door squeaked closed, the room became shadowy and eerie. Alice gasped when she caught sight of Doc, who'd donned his costume for the play.

The Ghost of Christmas Yet to Come was spooky, to say the least—and Doc had managed to make it even spookier by adding pale makeup to his face and dark eyeliner around his eyes.

"The Rizzo women did my makeup. What do you think?"

"Horrifying," said Owen.

"Good. That's just what we were going for," said Donna, coming into the room with Lafonda right behind her. Both were dressed in dark, hooded robes like Doc, but their base makeup had a ghastly green tinge to it.

"Eek!" said Owen, clapping. "You all look perfect!"

Dewey, who had arrived earlier, joined the group. "Okay, we're all set. I'll be listening from the sound booth at the back of the theater. If anyone needs anything, say the code word, uh . . . *Holly berries*. Okay?"

"Hey, if I need anything, I'm just going to scream

bloody murder, okay?" said Lafonda, putting her hands on her hips.

"Or that," said Dewey.

Doc chuckled. "I have no idea if this will suss out the killer, but either way, I'm glad to get out of the house. If I eat another bite of casserole, I'll explode." He pressed the button on the side of his watch to light it up. "We have to get this show on the road before the actual dress rehearsal for the play starts. Ethel Primrose is directing this year, and she runs a tight ship. You told our two suspects to come early, correct?"

"That's right," said Owen. "In fact, Dr. McCorkle will be here any minute. Places everyone!"

Everyone except for Owen and Dewey scuttled backstage, where Alice and Franny hid behind the big fan and snow machine that would be used for the closing scene of the play, when Ebenezer Scrooge, played by Granny's husband Chester Lehman, comes to his senses and changes his life for the better. It was the first year they'd been able to afford the snow machine—which they'd actually purchased with the proceeds from ticket sales the year before, and the whole town was excited about the big finale. Owen was stationed at the stage light control console, midway toward the back of the darkened theater.

Dewey could be heard jiggling the door to get into the sound booth at the very back.

"You have to yank it!" Owen called to him, after which they all heard the door bang open and then shut.

The stage was silent as the grave as they all waited in the dark for Samantha McCorkle to arrive. Alice could hear Franny nervously shifting her position. Alice had managed to sit down on the floor next to Franny but wasn't sure how she'd get up again. From their hiding place, she heard the side door in the kitchen open, then creak closed. Franny grabbed her arm and they waited.

"Hello?" Dr. McCorkle called out, jingling her keys. "Anyone in here?" She stood for a moment, then could be heard grumbling, "Owen James, you said six o'clock!" She turned to go, but then the spotlight which hung directly above Doc, who stood centerstage, snapped on. Dr. McCorkle turned to look at the stage.

The ghostly pale Doc stood there, flanked by his two ghoulish minions, the Rizzos. Alice couldn't see Doc's face—only his back—from her hiding place. But she could see Dr. McCorkle's face. Her eyes were wide and full of a mixture of shock and fear.

"It's me. Charles," Doc said in a half-groan.

Dr. McCorkle clutched her purse tightly. "You—you're dead."

"Yes. But not free yet. We have some unfinished business, Samantha."

Dr. McCorkle's expression transformed from fear to outrage. She began walking forward, and Alice lost sight of her as she swerved to the left. She and Franny both leaned sideways to see around the snow machine fan but didn't spot the doctor until she was on the stage, walking at top speed, an angry look on her face.

"You're darn right we have unfinished business!" she growled. "You cheated me out of that research position, and you know it, Charles Howard!" With that, she drew back and kicked Doc right in the shin.

"Ouch!" He bent over and grabbed his leg.

"There. *Now* our business is finished," said Dr. McCorkle, dusting off her hands. She stalked off the stage, pausing only once to say, over her shoulder, "Thank you, Doc. I needed that! I feel full closure now." With that she threw open the door and left the theater.

"That woman has a mean kick," said Doc, rubbing his shin. "And pointy shoes."

Owen came down the aisle. "Darn it! She recognized you, Doc. She didn't fall for our act."

"We had her going at the beginning, there," said Donna.

"Yeah," Lafonda agreed. "You could tell she was scared at first."

"There'll be heck to pay when I see her at the hospital," said Doc with a groan.

"Maybe we'd better regroup before Ms. Swift gets here," said Franny, coming out from behind the big fan.

Alice attempted to get to her feet but wobbled back and decided to stay put until someone could assist her. But before she had a chance to ask for help, the kitchen door could be heard opening and swinging shut.

"Oh no! She's early!" hissed Owen. "Hide!"

Luckily the spotlight was still on above Doc. The Rizzo sisters, who had stepped offstage, hesitated, not knowing what to do. Still at centerstage, Doc looked down at the floor, collecting himself. He cleared his throat.

Alice could hear Annabelle's gasp all the way from her spot behind the snow machine. She peeked around the side and saw Annabelle, walking slowly toward the stage, her face pale, her eyes wide. Doc spotted her and quickly turned away. Annabelle continued forward, taking the steps at stage right and walking up to Doc. A shiver ran down Alice's spine when she saw the look on Annabelle's face. She looked half-crazed—nothing like the calm and composed math teacher Alice had seen before.

"How is it that you're alive?" Annabelle asked, her voice low.

Doc cleared his throat, but only turned his face to the side, so that Annabelle could glimpse his hooded profile. His answer came out in a hoarse whisper. "I'm not. You killed me."

Annabelle laughed sharply at this. "You killed me first. It's only fair."

Doc started to walk away from her, but she reached out and just missed grabbing his arm.

"Did you hear me, Charles?" Her voice was trembling now. "You killed me that day when you broke it off! And letting everyone believe it was me who—who ended things between us? That didn't help at all! You thought you were being honorable!" she spat. "But *honorable* would've been keeping your commitment to me!"

Doc turned his head to the side again, and Alice could see his full face from where she sat. His eyes were huge.

Annabelle continued, "What I want to know is *why won't you just die*?" She lunged at Doc from behind, wrapped her arms around his neck, and began choking the life out of him. Alice did the first thing that came to mind, and flipped on the snow machine and fan, which began blowing puffy white flakes all over the stage. This sudden storm startled Annabelle enough that Doc was able to pry her arms away from his neck, and in the meantime, both the Rizzo sisters rushed forward and attacked Annabelle from the rear. Franny and Owen joined in the fight, and within a few seconds, Annabelle was contained, her arms pinned to her sides.

Dewey came running down the aisle, waving his handcuffs. "That darn door to the sound booth stuck again. But don't worry." He cuffed Annabelle's wrists. "I heard everything."

Franny and Owen came and found Alice, still sitting on the floor behind the snow machine, struggling to get to her feet.

"That sudden snowstorm was a stroke of genius," said Owen.

"Good," said Alice. "Now can someone please help me get up?"

CHAPTER 15

Ben and Luke managed to get back into town just as the Christmas dance was getting underway in Town Park that night. Alice had been standing in the gazebo with Mayor Abercrombie, who was welcoming everyone and making announcements about the upcoming week of festivities. The Gothic Trolls were already in place and waiting to kick off the dance. At the mayor's signal, they launched into a local favorite, their *Ballad of Mistletoe the Gnome*—a slow dance.

Franny, Owen, and Michael—who'd just returned home from his travels—were taking turns dancing Theo around under the thousands of twinkling holiday lights in the trees. Theo suddenly squealed with delight and pointed a pudgy finger. "Dada!" he said, his voice full of excitement.

Franny turned, spotted Ben, and ran to him. He swept her and Theo into his arms. Alice, from the gazebo, saw the commotion and caught the smiling eyes of her husband, who was looking beat, but handsome as ever as he walked toward her. He stopped at the bottom of the gazebo stairs and held out a hand. Alice grinned and took it, walking down the steps and right into his embrace.

"I'm sure there's some mistletoe around here somewhere," he said with a soft chuckle, planting a kiss on Alice's lips that she felt all the way down to her toes.

"Welcome home, Detective Evans," she said with a smile. "I missed you."

"Not as much as I missed you." He tucked an auburn curl behind her hear. "Dance with me?"

"If you don't mind that I'm a little wobbly," said Alice, glancing down at her belly.

"You've never been more beautiful, though." Luke guided her out to where the others were dancing.

As they swayed to that song and the next, Alice filled Luke in on the details of the investigation. He'd already heard it all from Dewey but wanted to get Alice's take.

Annabelle Swift had been unstable, even as a teenager when she and Charles Howard had fallen into tumultuous young love. They'd gotten engaged just after their high school graduation, then Charles went off to college, then medical school. He and Annabelle had kept the relationship alive from a distance through those years, and it wasn't until Charles returned home to Blue Valley that he'd spent consistent time with Annabelle.

That was when he'd realized there were problems with the relationship. Annabelle was at times very calm and amiable. She'd gotten her degree in education and kept an orderly classroom at the high school. But she was volatile and would fly into a rage at the drop of a hat in private. Charles had encouraged her to get counseling to no avail, and when his friend Samantha McCorkle told him about an opportunity opening up in New York, he had jumped at the chance to move away from the problematic relationship. He'd broken it off, but in an effort to spare Annabelle any embarrassment, had told everyone it was she who'd decided against getting married. Then he'd left town.

Annabelle had spotted Charles the same night Doc

had—the night of Alice's visit to the clinic. Annabelle had been out for a walk in the neighborhood, had seen Charles sneaking into the barn, and been horrified. That must've been when she'd snapped. She'd returned the following night—this time, with the intent to confront him. She'd brought the yearbook along, as well as the knife, to punish him for the heartbreak that had devasted her and that she'd never recovered from.

The pages that had been ripped from the book were recovered when her house was searched, and among the signatures from friends was a note from Charles, saying how they'd always be together and how his love for her would never die. As it turned out, she'd angrily ripped those pages out on that fateful night in the barn and had stuffed them into her pocket before running away after having stabbed Charles.

Annabelle confessed to the crime and Dewey and Trimble were praised for solving the case, even though Detective Evans and Captain Maguire were away. Of course, everyone in Blue Valley knew that the indomitable Alice, Owen, and Franny had probably had at least a little something to do with the outcome.

"Well done, junior detective," said Luke, twirling Alice on the grassy dancefloor. "Now. No more murders or investigations or mysteries or danger for a while, okay?"

"Don't worry," said Alice. "All I want to do now is enjoy the festival and celebrate the season. By the way, thanks for forcing half the town to come to my aid and volunteer for all the jobs this year. The week ahead is going to practically be a vacation for me."

Luke pulled back and frowned at her. "I can't take credit for that. But I'm glad to hear people have been stepping up."

Alice looked at him. "Are you *sure* you had nothing to do with the sudden influx of helpers?"

Luke held up a hand in pledge. "Absolutely sure." He pulled her close and they continued to dance.

Alice felt her heart swell, and a tear stung her eye. Resting her chin on Luke's shoulder, she looked around them. She could see Norman dipping Pearl Ann. Her mom and dad were dancing alongside Granny and Chester, who were cutting quite a rug. Franny's parents were getting their turn with Theo, allowing Franny to dance with Ben. Doc and Mrs. Howard were swaying to the music, talking and laughing with Marge and Koi. Even Ethel Primrose was twirling about from one dance partner to another. And finally, Idella Holcombe was dancing with her father, Willard, who had finally turned up late that afternoon. As it turned out, he'd been holed up in the storage room at Lucky's Quik Pik, subsisting on a diet of snack cakes and soda, and quite enjoying himself. These people had always come through for Alice. They were her extended family. She put an arm over her belly and smiled. These would be her little girl's family as well, and come spring, they would welcome her with the same love they'd always freely given to Alice.

She suddenly felt the Christmas spirit filling her heart in full force. Maybe it was the twinkling lights or the Gothic Trolls' holiday tunes. Maybe it was the sound of children's laughter coming from the faux ice rink, or the sight of Main Street beyond the park, all glittering and swagged in evergreen. Maybe it was the ancient snowcapped mountains watching over the valley. Or the thought of the cozy fireplace at the cabin on the lake, and how she and Luke would be decorating their Christmas tree this week—with Owen supplying plenty of cookies and Franny stringing the popcorn. Whatever it was that struck Alice so deeply that evening in the park, she'd never felt more grateful for the blessings that abounded in her life.

"Thank you," she whispered.

"What's that?" Luke looked at her, a little grin playing on his face.

"Hey you two!" Owen and Michael had wound their way through the crowd. "We're all going over to Franny and Ben's at the lake. We're going to read ""Twas the Night Before Christmas" to Theo and make paper chains for the tree. You coming?"

"Absolutely," said Alice.

"Sounds great," said Luke.

Owen slung an arm around Alice as they all walked toward the edge of the park. "Everyone's home, everyone's safe, and the festival is off to a fabulous start," he said. Then he sighed contentedly. "Merry Christmas, happy holidays, and God bless us every one!"

AUTHOR'S NOTE

I'd love to hear your thoughts on my books, the story-lines, and anything else that you'd like to comment on —reader feedback is very important to me. My contact information, along with some other helpful links, is listed on the next page. If you'd like to be on my list of "folks to contact" with updates, release and sales notifications, etc.... just shoot me an email and let me know. Thanks for reading!

Also...

... if you're looking for more great reads, Summer Prescott Books publishes several popular series by outstanding Cozy Mystery authors.

CONTACT SUMMER PRESCOTT BOOKS PUBLISHING

Blog and Book Catalog: http://summerprescottbooks.com
Email: summer.prescott.cozies@gmail.com

And…be sure to check out the Summer Prescott Cozy Mysteries fan page and Summer Prescott Books Publishing Page on Facebook – let's be friends!

To sign up for our fun and exciting newsletter, which will give you opportunities to win prizes and swag, enter contests, and be the first to know about New Releases, click here: http://summerprescottbooks.com

Made in the USA
Middletown, DE
29 August 2022

72548135R00076